For disclaimer, this is a work of fiction. All characters and places in this story are fictional, and any resemblance to persons living or dead is purely coincidental.

In the deep of worn and dirty rivers, mystery still flows.

Chapter 1: Playground

...: I grew up here as a kid... When I was older but still young, after I graduated for my doctorate, I left to go see the world... Being gone so long away from home, I never forgot its weather, its smell, its history, the people... No. Home never left me, no matter how long I was gone... There's something special about this place... Years later, I returned back home to Aqua Heights. Not a lot had changed. The only thing different now, is I'm living in old skin... But this place... Home... It has its ups and downs...

_____

_____

YEAR 1992

Somewhere up in the Poconos Mountains is a small town called Aqua Heights. A place that never leaves fall. It got its name from its uncommon disaster from the water plant that opened when the town was first built, and it grew a little over the years. Ever since the incident and after the plant being shut down, streams of boiling water still run underground to this day. The air always feels moist, the town is usually always wet, and the sky is always grey. People come and go, but it's always quiet. It's a peaceful place, but everywhere with light has darkness...

Later one day, Jonas and his daughter Eleanor are at Blue Creek Park. They are both happy and enjoying life together. They're down close by the waters of a river that passes by the town. The trees are hollow with orange and brown leaves as most of them covered the wet playground. They have the whole park to themselves as they play and bond freely. After the big slide, Eleanor tries the merry-go-round with her dad. Jonas spins her around, smiling big as she laughs hard with joy shining the day.

A little bit later, Jonas is pushing Eleanor on the swing-set. They're still the only ones at the park. The sounds of the rusted chains of the swings squeak at each push. Feeling the calm air on their faces, Jonas chats with his daughter.

Jonas: Hey? Can you spell your name?

Eleanor: E-L-E---A-N—O-R.

Jonas: How old are you?

Eleanor: 7.

Jonas: How old am I?

Eleanor: 40.

Jonas: What? I'm not 40. How old am I?

Eleanor: I don't know.

Jonas: Hmm. What's your favorite color?

Eleanor: Green.

Jonas: What's your favorite animal?

Eleanor: Elephants!

Jonas: Do you have an elephant?

Eleanor: Yes. But not a real one.

Jonas: What color is our house?

Eleanor: Yellow…

Jonas: You're so smart.

Eleanor: No. You are.

Jonas: Not as smart as you, princess. What do you want to be when you grow up?

Eleanor: An Astronaut!

As the two of them bonded more, Jonas's cell-phone started ringing.

Eleanor: Push me higher, daddy!

Jonas gives her a good push as he pulls out his phone. He sees his wife's name "Kim" on the small screen. He then answers the phone.

Jonas: Hey, honey.

Kim: Hey. I'm home early. Where are you and Eleanor?

Jonas: We're at the park.

Kim: Okay. Well, I'm going to go ahead and start making dinner.

Jonas: Okay. We'll be home soon. I love you, beautiful.

Kim: I love you, handsome.

They both hang up the conversation. Kim went to the kitchen to prepare early dinner for her family. Jonas is then ready to leave.

Jonas: Are you ready, kiddo? Your mom is making dinner.

Eleanor: I guess so.

Eleanor jumps out of the swing and walks beside Jonas as he puts his arm around her. They both leave the park together. Captured in focused lenses, they get inside a 1978 baby blue Sky-Bird. Jonas starts up the car as he and Eleanor put on their seatbelts. Driving on the wet pavement, they leave the park for the day, and they head home.

Later on the road to home, close to evening, the sky remains with grey clouds. Parts of the broken soil from some of the hills are constantly releasing steam fogs. The tires of the car are splashing little mists of water from the asphalt. Eleanor is tuned in on Jonas's radio that is static with some law enforcement mentioning a homicide. She was curious.

Eleanor: What's a homicide?

Jonas then realizes that his daughter was listening to the horrors being told. He turns the volume down, eventually turning it off.

Jonas: Now. You don't need to be listening to that.

Eleanor: Why?

Jonas: Because that's grown-up stuff...

Eleanor didn't argue, but she wondered what was so bad about what she was listening to that her dad didn't want her to hear. Jonas then comes up with a solution as he turns on the stereo.

Jonas: How about some music?

Eleanor: Yeah!

Jonas pulls out a mix-tape from the center console and places it inside the tray to play. It starts playing track 1.

Jonas: There we go. My baby blue.

The two of them sit back and listen to the classic rock playing in the car on the rest of the way home.

A little bit later, on track 5, they're pulling up in the gravel driveway of their home on a small wooded hillside at the edge of town. The car is parked and is turned off. Jonas and Eleanor both get out and head towards the front door on the open porch. Eleanor runs ahead of Jonas with excitement to be home.

Eleanor: Mommy!

Eleanor starts running towards her mom in the kitchen giving her a big warm hug.

Kim: Hey, princess! Did you have fun at the park today?

Eleanor: Yeah! We had the park all to ourselves!

Kim: You did?! That must've been fun!

Shortly after, Jonas starts walking in the house and into the kitchen.

Kim: Hey, honey.

Jonas: Hey. So work let you off early?

Kim: Yeah. Mary wanted to start her shift early, so I let her.

Jonas: Well, I'm glad.

Kim: Me too. Dinner is ready by the way. Are you two hungry?

Eleanor: Arghh! I'm so hungry!

Jonas laughs a little at their daughter's response.

Jonas: Yes. We're starving.

Kim: Alright. Go ahead and sit. I'll get the plates.

Both Jonas and Eleanor sit at the table in the dining room while Kim made their plates. After setting up the table, she sits down and joins them. The three of them then enjoy a meal together as a family for the first time in a while.

Later after dinner, Jonas just finished helping Eleanor with her homework. Kim is in the kitchen hand-washing the dirty dishes that were piled up from the last few days. At this point it was getting close to bedtime.

Jonas: Alright, missy. It's time for you to go brush your teeth and start getting ready for bed.

Eleanor: Okay, daddy.

Eleanor runs along down the hallway to the bathroom as Kim watches her pass by, smiling to herself. Jonas watches her from the dining room table, feeling at peace and happiness as he then stands up and walks over to Kim. He kisses her on the head and steps in on doing the dishes.

Jonas: I got the rest of these, honey.

Kim: Okay. I'm gonna give her a bath. I love you.

Jonas: I love you.

Kim softly rubs Jonas's back as she leaves him to the rest of the dishes to spend more time with Eleanor.

Later that night, Eleanor is in her bed about to go to sleep. Jonas stands up from the bed, moving a few strands of hair from her face.

Eleanor: Goodnight, daddy.

Jonas: Goodnight, baby girl.

He leaves the lamp on for her comfort, and he leaves the room closing the door behind him. Once she went to sleep, he went to the master bathroom to find his wife standing in front of the mirror with her night robe on. Jonas walks behind her, softly wrapping his arms around her, holding her close as he kisses her on her neck. After feeling the warm touch, Jonas gets in the shower.

A little bit later, the water from the shower steamed up the room. Jonas is relaxed, feeling the warm water on his head. The sliding door then opens with Kim stepping inside to join him. Enjoying a shower together, they hold each other close. Not having their time together in a while made the moment more special. Kim and Jonas both look at each other without saying a word, knowing that they're both happy and they wouldn't change anything. Kim then slowly leans in, giving the first kiss to her husband as he gives back. They continue kissing each other genuinely, and they kiss each other more. One thing led to another that night.

Early the next morning, everyone is in the dining room. Kim and Jonas are enjoying their coffee as Eleanor enjoyed her pancakes. It's about time to head out the door.

Kim: It's supposed to rain a little this afternoon. Both of you take your raincoats.

Jonas: Alright. Are you ready to go?

Eleanor: Yeah.

Jonas: Okay. Grab your backpack and coat, and give your mom a kiss.

Eleanor grabs both of her things and gives her mom a kiss. Jonas then gives his wife a kiss before they head out the door.

Later after driving from home, Jonas is dropping Eleanor off at school.

Jonas: Have a good day at school! Give me a kiss.

Eleanor kisses Jonas on the cheek before exiting the car. He rolls the window down as she's walking to the front door of her school.

Jonas: I love you!

She turns around and smiles with a response.

Eleanor: Love you!

Jonas watches Eleanor, making sure she made it inside before driving off to work.

Later today at Jonas's work, he's been stuck at his desk with paperwork all day. Unit chief Cyndy walks by and sits on the desk.

Cyndy: Hey, Jonas.

Jonas: Chief.

Cyndy: Please. Just Cyndy... It's been about 2 years since Danny left, and you're the only one who still respects me.

Jonas: Well, Danny and I both knew you deserved the position. Deep down, I think we all did.

Cyndy: Hmph. Those assholes just don't wanna admit it. Like they do any work. They're all probably down at the pony.

Jonas: Yeah. That's why you're the boss and they're not.

Cyndy: You're damn right.

They both laugh a little, then Jonas starts getting back to work.

Cyndy: Hey. Don't worry about that paperwork. I'll make Hotch do it.

Jonas: Are you sure?

Cyndy: Yeah. They don't have to like me, but I am their boss. I've got a case-file for you.

Cyndy then hands Jonas the file and he starts to open it.

Cyndy: How's training going?

Jonas: It's alright. I can't wait to be done with it though.

Cyndy: Well, you know they're going to be working with you. Right?

Jonas: Cyndy. I don't know. I don't want someone that's gonna end up half-assing things.

Cyndy: That's why I put him with you... He won't. I know you.

Jonas: Alright. I just hope you know what you're doing.

Cyndy: That's why I'm chief.

Jonas sits back in his chair looking at his desk as Cyndy gets up.

Cyndy: Would you look at that case before you leave?

Jonas: Yes ma'am.

Cyndy: Don't ever call me ma'am again. We're friends. And don't forget that I'm the one that trained you.

Jonas laughs a little more at Cyndy's seriousness as she walks off. He then takes a look at the case-file she handed to him. It's the murder of two children, Andrew and April.

ANDREW'S FILE:

Age: 8

Weight: 57lbs

Height: 50.8"

Hair Color: Light Brown

Reading into Andrew's file, his body was found in a dumpster behind Niko's Bowl-N-Pins, two days after he went missing. The case explains that Andrew was protecting his 11 year old sister, April.

APRIL'S FILE:

Age: 11

Weight: 80lbs

Height: 55.7"

Hair Color: Dark Brown

April was abducted, and two weeks later her body was found in the woods nearby White Lake. Both Andrew and April were stabbed to death, and they were both left holding a Lilium flower.

Jonas: Lilies?

Looking deeper into the case and reading more about the children, it brings a sad memory to Jonas. Their pictures definitely brought him back to when he was a child.

_____

_____

YEAR 1968

Around 11 o'clock at night, Jonas is with his mother Amelia in some dead parking lot. Jonas is only 5 years old, and is out in the cold as Amelia is talking to some stranger in a car. After a small chat, Amelia speaks to her son.

Amelia: Jonas. I need you to face this way and cover your ears.

Jonas: Where are you going, mommy?

Amelia: Nowhere, baby. This is a game. Mommy's gotta do something for a minute. If you're good, I'll get you an early birthday present. Would you like that?

Jonas: Yes.

Amelia: Okay. Remember. Look this way, and don't move until I tell you to.

Jonas: Okay.

Jonas is left outside in the cold as Amelia gets inside the car with the stranger. He is facing away with his ears covered as Amelia starts having sex in the backseat. While playing the game, her son does the best he can to muffle out the sounds.

Early the next day, in room 321 at Bloom-Weather Apartments, Jonas is home asleep. He's then awakened by Amelia.

Amelia: Hey, handsome! How'd you sleep?

Jonas: Good.

Amelia: I got you a present!

Jonas is more awake with excitement as his loving mother pulls out the gift. The present is a new stuffed blue elephant.

Amelia: Do you like it?

Jonas: Yes! Thanks, mommy!

Jonas grabs the stuffed animal and hugs it tight, feeling the soft material against his skin. In their sweet little moment, it is then interrupted. Some knocking is heard at the door. Amelia gets up and goes to check who it is. She looks out through the peephole and sees what looks to be bad news. Amelia then opened the door seeing the landlord with social services, accompanied by two police officers. The social worker then speaks.

Harper: Hi. I'm Harper. I'm with social services. Are you Amelia Rivers?

Amelia: What is this?

Her landlord Ronnie then speaks his doings.

Ronnie: You haven't paid rent for the last 2 months.

Amelia: I said you'd get your money!

Ronnie: That was 3 weeks ago when you asked me for another extension! I've been very patient and very generous with you!

Amelia: Ronnie, please. I need more time.

Ronnie: I'm sorry, Amelia. I can't wait any longer.

Amelia didn't know what she was going to do as she had no other options at this point.

Harper: Ms. Rivers? I've already talked to Mr. Wallace. He's willing to let us help you keep your place. But until you can keep a stable home, we still have concerns for your child... Is Jonas here?

Jonas then steps out from their little hall with his little elephant. Harper then steps inside their apartment and walks over to Jonas. Amelia is worried sick for them.

Harper: Hi, Jonas. My name is Harper. I'm with social services. I work with children.

Jonas didn't speak at first as he can sense that something was wrong.

Jonas: What're you gonna do?

Harper: I'm gonna try to help you and your mom. Okay?

Amelia looks more concerned as Harper spoke with Jonas. Harper then looks at Amelia, and back to focus on Jonas.

Harper: Jonas? Would you mind to come with me?

Jonas didn't know how to react as Harper started gently guiding him alongside her.

Amelia: What're you doing?!

The two officers start stepping in Amelia's path as Harper walks by with Jonas, trying to ignore her.

Amelia: Where are you taking him?!

The officers grabbed Amelia's arms as she tried approaching Harper. Jonas then turns back, looking at his mother in confusion and worry.

Jonas: Mom?!

Ronnie stepped aside from the doorway, letting Harper and Jonas pass through into the hallway. Amelia grows angrier with anxiety and struggle as the officers keep her from her son.

Amelia: Where are you taking him?!! You can't just take my son away from me!! AAAAAAAAAHHHHHHHHH!!!!!!!!

Amelia became more violent with the officers as she screams louder and louder from losing her son. Jonas could hear his mother screaming with pain and frustration as he's walking with Harper down the long hallway. He is still holding the blue elephant his mother got for him, being the last piece of her he had. After being taken away, everything else was a blur moment fading into white.

The small memory faded back into time at Jonas's work. Jonas sat still, remembering his last moments with his mother. He looks back at the case file, putting it back together and taking it with him before leaving his desk. Jonas walks into Cyndy's office taking another gander at the file. He had a theory.

Cyndy: What do you have for me, agent Jonas?

Jonas: Cyndy. I don't think the boy was supposed to be killed.

Cyndy: You think he was in the way?

Jonas: Well, the boy was only missing for 2 days until he was found. The girl was taken and missing for almost 3 weeks.

Cyndy: Meaning, she was the target.

Jonas: Yes. And April was probably still alive. Andrew just made things more difficult, so the suspect had to act quickly. Also, I think the lilies are a sign of remorse.

Cyndy: The boy was left in a dumpster. They didn't have time at the moment. They would've had to go back later to pay their respects.

Jonas: The question I still have is what was their reason for keeping April alive? She was taken, and she was alive for 2 weeks. But there were no signs of abuse or rape. Why wait so long just to kill her?

Cyndy: Hopefully we'll find out, once we find out who did it.

Cyndy then grabs her purse and starts getting a few other things together to leave.

Cyndy: Alright. Well, I'm out of here for today. Are you?

Jonas: Yeah. I gotta go pick up my daughter from school.

Cyndy: Ah, I love kids. I just don't know if I could handle any of my own.

Jonas: What do you mean? You already do at work.

Referring to the entire department, they both laugh a little.

Cyndy: Yeah. Well, you already see how that's going. Anyways, I gotta get going.

Jonas: Alright. I'll look more into this tonight.

Cyndy: Let me know what you find tomorrow morning. Have a good night, Jonas.

Jonas: You too, Cyndy.

Cyndy walks off, leaving the department as Jonas grabs his things to do the same.

A little bit later, after leaving the station, Jonas pulls up at Milford Elementary School to pick up his daughter. The rain is already coming down as Eleanor gets in the car.

Jonas: Hey, sweetie. Did you have a good day at school, today?

Eleanor: Yeah. Hey, daddy? Can we go to the park?

Jonas: Eleanor, it's raining. Plus, I'm really tired. I don't have the energy.

Eleanor: I have my raincoat and my rain boots.

Jonas: Another day, Ellie. Okay?

Eleanor: Okay.

Eleanor is a little disappointed, but she didn't say more to her dad.

A few minutes later, Jonas keeps glancing over at Eleanor. She's staring out the passenger window in silence looking at the rain. As Jonas kept his eyes on the road and would occasionally check on his daughter, he started feeling bad for her. In thought to himself, he takes a turn to surprise her.

A little bit later on the road, they pull up at Blue Creek Park. Just as Jonas planned, Eleanor is surprised.

Eleanor: You said we weren't going to the park.

Jonas: Yeah. I know. Your mother's going to be upset with me keeping you out in this weather. Come on.

Eleanor is excited to go play at the park again as the rain falls steadily. The air is fogged a little by the rain and the steam rising from the ground. Jonas and Eleanor are in their raincoats, walking on the sidewalk by the river towards the park. On their way there as they got closer, Jonas is suddenly struck at the back of the head with a blunt object, knocking him down to the wet pavement unconscious. Eleanor screams from the trauma, seeing her dad on the ground, bleeding from his head.

Eleanor: Daddy?!!

Jonas barely moved a muscle as he could just feel the cold rain and the warm blood on his skin. Eleanor is then grabbed by the unknown perpetrator, making her scream and calling out to her dad.

Eleanor: Dad!! Daddy!! Help me, daddy!!! Daddy!!!

Jonas struggled to move as the voice of his daughter fades further out by the rain, then there was nothing but ringing in his ears. His vision became a blur and his eyes closed. With no one around to help Jonas, he lies in the rain on the hard concrete as the blood from his head streamed down his face.

Chapter 2: 6 Years Later

6 YEARS LATER

YEAR 1998

At this current time, Jonas is living at old Bloom-Weather. Six lonely years have passed for Jonas as him and Kim had divorced, after Eleanor. After three decades, the building is more rundown than it was before. It's close to the middle of the day as Jonas starts to get up from his loud squeaking bed as he's aching all over from various things. The day had stayed in bed with him. His room is in a depressing state; it's dull and dark with the light of day barley shining through the blinds. His home phone that's lying on the nightstand had a new voicemail. The voicemail then plays itself. It was Cyndy who had left a message.

Cyndy: Hey, Jonas. It's Cyndy… I wanted to check in on you. I hope you're doing okay… Listen. I know it's around that time of the year, and I know it's hard for you… I just want to tell you to take as much time off as you need. And I also wanted to see if you wanted to maybe have coffee together, sometime? Think about it… I'll keep checking up on you. Okay? Take care, Jonas.

The message ends and the ceiling fan is then the only sound present as Jonas sits on the edge of the bed, feeling the cool air on his skin. He then gets up and walks to the bathroom. Flipping on the light switch, standing in front of the mirror, Jonas appeared tired with his baggy eyes and scruffy beard. After opening the mirror cabinet, he took some pain killers. He then turns on the sink, splashing cold water in his face and rubbing it in his hair to wake him up. Once he had freshened himself up a little, he wanders into the kitchen. Other than his bedroom, everything else almost seemed untouched. Jonas walks past a happy photo of him and Eleanor at White Lake, ignoring it as he makes him a cup of old coffee. Taking a drink of the warmed up coffee, he walks into the living room and takes a look out the dusty windows. Nothing was out of the ordinary as he just sees some of the neighbors living their normal lives. Some kids are playing in the courtyard and Jonas would occasionally hear his neighbors from next door. He then steps away from the windows and sits down on the couch. While drinking the rest of his coffee, he sees what's on TV. Jonas is flipping through the channels as nothing was on; the old speaker of the TV is mostly filled with static. A few seconds later, his cell-phone buzzes. He got a small text from his partner, Zach.

Text From Zach:

Zach: Hey, we got another case, if you want to take a look?

Jonas read the message but didn't respond. He listened to the static of the TV before turning it off. Jonas then gets up from the couch and sets his cup on the kitchen counter; he then puts on a coat before leaving his apartment. Stepping out of his room 320, he stops and sees the room 321 across from him. No one has been living in that room for a while; it's just a constant reminder of his past. He then moves on down the dark hall to leave.

Later on the same day, further up in the mountain hills at an abandoned train is where another body was found. The grey clouded sky broke with quiet thunder as the slow wind blows off brown leaves from the trees and a small cliff-side onto the old rusted train and the railroad tracks. After Jonas pulled up, he got out of his car to join the crime scene. His partner Zach meets up with him to bring him up to speed.

Zach: Hey, Jonas. I'm glad you could make it.

Jonas: Do you have the file?

Zach: Right here.

Zach then hands Jonas the file, containing the info on a girl named Eirene.

EIRENE'S FILE:

Age: 12

Weight: 92lbs

Height: 61.0"

Hair Color: Blonde

After looking at the file, Zach fills him in on the rest.

Zach: Her parents reported her missing a few days ago when she didn't come home from school.

Jonas: Where is she now?

Zach looks over at the corroded black train in an answer to Jonas. They then both walk to the train, heading inside one of the old passenger cars. The car is filled with dust and CSI collecting evidence for forensics. Eirene's body is lying in the middle of the walkway with a white sheet draped over her. Cyndy is also there overseeing and investigating. She then meets with Jonas and Zach.

Cyndy: Agent Jonas. I'm glad you're here with us. Agent Zach?

Zach: Chief Cyndy. I've only given Jonas little details with the case.

Cyndy: Well, that's about all we have for now, unfortunately. What we do know, is Eirene died from multiple stab wounds. She was found by some young kids exploring out here.

Jonas then walks over to Eirene's body, moving the sheet a little to find her holding a lily. The lily flower is what stood out to him more than anything. He lays the sheet back down, feeling numb to the sight as he sits down in one of the old seats by the dirty stained window.

Jonas: This has to be tied with the other cases that went cold a few years back.

Cyndy: Yes. Which is why those cases are being re-opened.

Zach: Do you think it's our same guy?

Cyndy: Well, there's nothing different about their M.O. It could be a copycat, but it's unlikely.

Jonas then gets up from the seat speaking with hidden disgust.

Jonas: It's the same guy. The only thing different is the girl's age. She's older; so to them, they gained more confidence. The coward only preys on innocent children.

The three of them then leave the passenger car of the train and discuss further.

Cyndy: I think we've done all we can do here. I'm heading back to the station. Why don't you both head over to where Eirene went to school, and see if you can find any more info there.

Zach: Yes, ma'am.

Cyndy made no comment as she walks to her car and leaves to head back to the station. Jonas then gets in his car as Zach gets in on the passenger side.

Zach: What was that all about?

Jonas: She doesn't like being called ma'am.

Zach: Oh... Whoops.

Jonas then shifts the gears of the car, and they leave.

Later at Wateredge Middle School, Zach is outside of the main doors finishing up with one of the faculties.

Zach: Thank you for your time. You have a good day.

Zach then walks back down the steps back to Jonas's car and gets inside.

Jonas: Anything?

Zach: No. Nobody saw anyone that they didn't recognize. She might've walked home. They could've easily followed her without looking suspicious.

Jonas gives no further response as him and Zach leave the middle school.

Later at the end of the day, everyone started getting ready to leave work. Zach walks past Jonas at his desk, and he speaks to him on his way out.

Zach: Hey. You and I need to hang out again sometime. It's been too long.

Jonas: Yeah. Maybe.

Zach: You just let me know. Alright? I'm a phone call away. Have a good night, Jonas.

Jonas: Thanks, Zach. You too.

Zach then leaves the department as Jonas starts putting his stuff together for the day. Cyndy is then walking by and stops to talk.

Cyndy: Hey, Jonas. How are you?

Jonas: I am sure you already know, Cyndy.

Cyndy: How's Kim? Have you talked to her at all?

Jonas: No. We haven't talked since…

Cyndy: I'm sorry. That was stupid of me.

Jonas: It's okay.

Cyndy: Look. I know it's a little late for coffee, but I wanted to ask if you still wanted to join me for some drinks.

Jonas: Drinks with the boss? That sounds risky.

Cyndy: Nah. It'll be just friends who are off duty having a good time.

Jonas: I don't know if I really should, Cyndy.

Cyndy: Okay. I just thought that you might want some company. Goodnight, Jonas.

Cyndy then walks away to leave as Jonas stood back at his desk for a moment, feeling a little bad from his choice.

Later that night, Jonas had already made it home. He sits on the couch in the living-room alone looking at a small printed photo of him with his old family, Kim and Eleanor. Jonas stared at the photo every night as a reminder of what he had before and the guilt he carries with him. After looking at the photo of his family, he then picks up his cell. Looking at the name Cyndy, he hesitates for a moment, and then proceeds to call. The dial rings as he waits patiently, and she then answers his call.

Jonas: Hey...

Even later, after Jonas had called Cyndy, while he's sitting in the living room watching TV he hears a few knocks at his door. He gets up from the couch and walks over to the door. He then looks out the peephole to see who it was and realizes it's his company. Jonas then opens the door to see Cyndy standing in the hall smiling delicately at him.

Cyndy: Hey... May I come in?

Jonas: Please.

Jonas steps aside with his manners, letting Cyndy enter the apartment. He looks at the room 321 for just a moment before closing the door.

A few hours have passed, and Cyndy and Jonas are both still visiting together. In the living room they're sitting on the couch, some Chinese takeout and a big bottle of wine is sitting on the coffee table in front of them. They've already had a few drinks but still have the giggles and chatting going.

Cyndy: Do you remember that one night when we arrested that guy who was drunk on a scooter?

Jonas snickers a little from his remembrance.

Jonas: Yeah. That was down by Coda River.

Cyndy: God. I miss those days.

Jonas then takes another drink of his wine as Cyndy follows after him.

Jonas: Thanks for coming over tonight.

Cyndy: Of course. If you ever need to talk, I'm here. Or if you ever want to drink some more wine and have Chinese again, I'm all for it.

Cyndy gets closer to Jonas, placing her hand on his lap without knowing her own actions.

Cyndy: We're friends, Jonas.

Jonas looks over at Cyndy, and they lock eyes for while. The feelings between them were tense for a moment then released in time. Without any hesitation, without any thought, neither one of them hold back as they then kiss each other. After feeling their soft passion and comfort of one another they kept it going, not wanting that feeling to stop. And not wanting the night to end, their actions end up leading to another.

_____

_____

Very early the next morning, while it's still dark out, Cyndy is already up getting dressed. Jonas is barely awake on the couch as he notices Cyndy putting on the rest of her clothes.

Jonas: Hey... You can use my bathroom to freshen up if you need to? Can I make you something to eat?

Cyndy: That's okay. I need to head home before going to work. Next time we'll do this sort of thing at my place.

Jonas: Next time?

Cyndy: I don't know. I'm sorry about last night. Last night was... I needed it... And I know you did too... This doesn't have to be something, Jonas. Or anything. But I have to go. Maybe I'll see you at work?

Jonas: Yeah, maybe…

Cyndy then grabs her purse and starts to walk out the door.

Jonas: Cyndy?… Thank you… really…

Cyndy: Sure thing…

She then continues out the door and walks down the hall to the stairway exit.

A little bit later, Jonas had shaved the scruff off his face and is now getting out of the shower. After cleaning himself up, he started getting dressed. He then steps out into the hallway of his apartment, putting on a jacket and grabbing his car keys from the kitchen counter. Before leaving, he notices a folded piece of paper that someone had slid underneath his door sometime earlier. It seemed strange, and with question and curiosity he picks up the piece of paper. When he unfolded it, it read his daughter's name "From E.L.E.A.N.O.R." The two words are written in crayon, each letter a different color and her name abbreviated like it's being spelled. Jonas's heart is already racing, but even more worry comes to him when he sees a drawing of a lily below the words. He then opens the door and looks out into the hall in both directions. No one was in sight, and all he could wonder is if his daughter is still alive.

Later, after getting the mysterious paper concerning Jonas's daughter, he makes it to work to bring it up with Cyndy. Feeling anxious, he doesn't waste any time as he's walking fast through the department. Jonas then starts to pass up Zach along the way.

Zach: Hey. Jonas. Can you take a look at this real quick—

Jonas: Not now.

Zach: What? It'll just take a second—

Jonas: I said, not now! Zach!

Zach: Yeah, sure. Okay? No problem.

Jonas continued on as Zach watches him feeling curious and concerned for Jonas. He then walks into Cyndy's office, quickly closing the door behind him. Cyndy is just finishing up a call as it didn't take her long to notice his presence. She then hangs up the phone to see what is going on.

Cyndy: Hey, Jonas. What is it—

Jonas immediately places the piece of paper onto her desk in showing his concern. Cyndy knew what this was without explanation.

Jonas: I found this at my door, after you left!

Cyndy: Did you see anybody leave this?

Jonas: No! Cyndy! But the son of a bitch that we've been looking for has my daughter!

Jonas is slowly breaking down inside as Cyndy takes a breath and tries to keep things calm.

Cyndy: Jonas. We don't know if it's the same guy—

Jonas: Promise me! Promise me that you'll help me look into this!

Cyndy: ... I promise...

Jonas is looking Cyndy in the eye with desperation of wanting to find his daughter. He then steps away feeling the stress and torment coming back to him as he tries to think about what to do next. During his thought, Cyndy speaks to him.

Cyndy: Jonas. I know this is a lot on you. But just go back home and try to get some rest—

Jonas: Get some rest?! I need to find who took my daughter!

Cyndy: And not clearing your head isn't going to help. Trust me. Okay? We're going to find this guy… I'll check up on you, later.

Jonas feels congested with anxiety and lost in his own mind. He leaves Cyndy's office without further intrusion. As he's about to leave he's walking past Zach again.

Zach: Jonas? Hey? What's going on? What's happening with you?

Jonas: Eleanor is alive…

Zach looks a little shocked and confused from what Jonas had said with nothing else to say. Walking past him again, Jonas leaves the department building to go back to his old home.

The grey cloudy skies barley show any movement, steam rises from underneath the dirt every now and then. Sometime later, at Jonas's old home, Kim is inside moving things around. She was busy with boxing some personal things and doing some small painting, and then she hears the doorbell ring. Kim stops what she's doing to go see who's at the door. When she opens the door she is surprised to see her ex-husband standing in front of her looking worse than when she last saw him.

Jonas: Hey. Kim…

Kim: What're you doing here, Jonas?

Jonas: Kim. I need to show you something.

Kim: What?

Jonas then pulls out the wrinkled paper that he got this morning and hands it to Kim. She looks at the writing, reading her daughter's name but she didn't know what it meant.

Kim: What is this?

Jonas: A note that I got this morning. I think that Eleanor is alive. I know she is.

Kim: Jonas. Please. Some kids probably did this as a prank—

Jonas: No, Kim! This isn't a prank! I don't know how, but I know she's still out there somewhere! I can feel it!

Kim: Stop it. Stop it!

Jonas: Kim! The flower on the note is a sign that the person who took our daughter was the same one who killed those children years ago!

Kim: Jonas, stop it!! Stop it!! Eleanor has been missing for 6 years! She's gone! You need to accept that!

Jonas felt more angry and betrayed by Kim's words and her lack of hope for Eleanor still being alive. He stood still for a moment before coming back to say his words.

Jonas: No. No, I won't accept that. I can't accept that. Not now… I'm gonna find her, Kim. I'm gonna fix this…

Kim: You need to leave. And you should see someone… Goodbye, Jonas…

In Kim's denial and sadness, she closes the door on Jonas. He stood there in thought as things didn't go the way he had hoped. Jonas then walks away to his car. Kim is in a little bit of distress after her unsuspecting visit. She then walks down the hallway of her lonely home past some old family photos of the three of them on the walls. Kim comes across Eleanor's room, and she opens the door stepping inside for the first time in a while. Purple and pink decorated walls and stuffed animals on the bed, nothing had changed. The room was untouched by the absence of their daughter, and as Kim is sitting on the bed a lot of old painful memories came back. She then started crying alone in Eleanor's room, and Jonas is still in the driveway in his car with hesitation. Without any further thoughts, he starts his car, and as he's looking at his old home in concern for Kim he drives away.

Later that night, Jonas is at the local bar "Heaven's Cup." He's sitting at the counter to himself looking at the small piece of paper. Shortly then, Hugo the bartender comes his way.

Hugo: Need anything more, Jonas?

Jonas: Another amaretto sour. Please.

Hugo then takes Jonas's empty glass for another refill. An older man then decides to join beside Jonas.

...: I'll have whatever he's having!

The man sits down in the stool next to him giving him unwanted company.

...: Hello. I walked in and saw you sitting over here by yourself. I thought I'd join you... My name's Walter.

Jonas: Hello. Walter.

Hugo comes back with their drinks and places them in front of them.

Jonas: Thanks, Hugo.

Walter: Yes. Thank you, sir.

Hugo: Sure thing, gentlemen.

Jonas and Walter were then left to their drinks.

Walter: Thank god it wasn't scotch. That stuff is worse than drinking piss… I used to be a bartender, long ago. I used to be a lot of things. Now, I'm just an old man waiting for the time to pass by.

Jonas just kept ignoring the old man, but Walter isn't as dumb as he looks.

Walter: You know? I can tell you're upset about something… Yes. Even an old guy like me can notice it.

Jonas: Listen, buddy. I don't wanna talk to anybody. Can you give me some space?

Walter: Sure… "Candy is dandy, but liquor is quicker." Here's to you, Gene.

Walter then quickly downs his drink, and hollers at the bartender.

Walter: Hey, Hugo! This is for the drinks! And a little something for you too!

Walter puts his money on the counter in payment for the drinks and a tip for the bartender. After paying in full and then extra, he starts to leave.

Walter: Maybe next time we have a drink together it'll be some vodka. Take care, young man.

Walter then leaves the tavern with no words from Jonas. However, Jonas definitely appreciated the old man's generosity. Jonas then chugs down the rest of his drink, feeling it all at once. He's playing with the empty glass of ice as the bartender walks back over collecting the money.

Hugo: That old-timer seems like a nice guy.

Jonas: Yeah… Here's something from me too. Thanks for the drink.

Hugo: Have a good night, Jonas.

After leaving a tip, since the old man had already paid for the drinks he leaves the bar for the night.

A little bit later, Jonas is in the parking lot getting out of his car and walking towards the apartments in the rain. Inside where it's dry, under the fluorescent lights down the hall, Jonas makes it to his room. Just as he's unlocking his door, Cyndy shows up at the right time. Her arms are full of groceries.

Jonas: Hey?

Cyndy: Hey. I thought I could fix you something, tonight.

Jonas: Well, that would be just great. What did you have in mind?

Cyndy: Chicken and dumplings.

Jonas: Oh, I'm looking forward to that.

Cyndy: Good. 'Cause I make a lot of it.

They both enter into Jonas's apartment, getting away from the world. Cyndy sets the sack of groceries on the kitchen counter and starts getting things ready for dinner.

Jonas: Do you know where everything's at?

Cyndy: If I don't, it won't be hard to find.

Jonas: Alright. If you don't mind, I'm going to take a shower.

Cyndy: It's your place. Just don't get wet.

Jonas smirks as he wonders off leaving Cyndy to her cooking.

Moments later, the showerhead gives away water. Steam starts rising up to the ceiling and fogging up the small room. Jonas stands below the hot water feeling it all wash over him after a long day. Deep in thought to himself, Jonas starts feeling nostalgic thinking back to him and Kim. He remembers her love, her touch; he remembered that special moment they had to each other. Finding himself under the water alone, he sighs as he closed his eyes trying to forget his demons. Flashbacks of him being taken away from his mother and his daughter being taken woke him back up.

After Jonas was out of the shower and had gotten dressed, he joined Cyndy in the living room. The food in the bowls are steaming hot on the coffee table.

Jonas: That smells good.

Cyndy: Well, there'll be plenty more leftover for you.

Jonas sits down on the couch beside her with a soft appreciation.

Jonas: You don't have to do this… You know that. Right?

Cyndy: I know you, Jonas. And I'm not giving up on this… On you…

Jonas: What about Eleanor?

Cyndy: I'm not…

Jonas thinks to himself for a moment, feeling a little better after taking everything in.

Jonas: This. This really is great... Thank you.

They both dig in, enjoying the food and their company together as the night went by.

After dinner, Cyndy leaves heading out into the hallway to go home this time. Once she left, Jonas turns around and starts to cleanup, gathering some of the dishes into the sink.

At this time, Zach is at his own place looking over the case files to study over. While looking them over, he looks at the lily flowers left with each victim, trying to come to conclusions.

Late at night, Walter just finished typing things up on his computer. His best friend, a black Labrador is at his side. Leaving the work office, they both walk down the hallway of their home for bed.

Elsewhere, on the wet roads in Aqua Heights, Cyndy is in her car on her way home. While driving through the steamy air with her headlights blinding in the night, she looks over at the passenger seat. Cyndy is then looking at her gun and her badge as in why she even took this job as her feelings for Jonas seem to be getting the best of her.

Back at the home that used to be nirvana, Kim is still moving things around. She is currently going through boxes of old things. One memory caught her eye as she pulls it out of the box, seeing a picture of her and Jonas's wedding in 1984.

At Bloom-Weather, Jonas is in the kitchen holding onto the picture of him and Eleanor at White Lake. Without a doubt in his mind, he knows his daughter is still alive. No one could tell him otherwise.

Jonas: I'll find you, baby. I promise…

Taking a long lasting look at the photo in high hopes, he goes to his room. Jonas then turns on the light on the nightstand and sits on the edge of the bed as he takes the mysterious note he got that morning. He looks at the note, reading his daughter's name and wanting answers, hoping she's alright, hoping she's okay. With nothing more to see, he puts the note back on the nightstand, turning the light off as he lies down to try and get some sleep.

Chapter 3: Blink of A Dream

Down the quiet halls of Bloom-Weather Apartments, in Jonas's room, he's lying in bed asleep. The hollow walls breathe heavily. His mind plays tricks on him. He can hear the sounds of rusted metal scraping against each other as he hears his own heartbeat. Jonas then hears the faded and distorted moans of the dead victims outside his apartment. His heart starts pounding harder, and he began hearing loud banging outside his door. The ceiling is low and flooded with upside down water dripping onto Jonas and the molded floor. Outside all the windows is nothing but brick walls. He started having flashbacks again of his mother, but she's visually different as her appearance is inhuman. Jonas starts tightening up in fear of his demons. His heart beats faster. Eleanor speaks in his head over and over to the last time they were together.

Eleanor: Daddy!!

Jonas could feel it all over again in replay. He could feel the back of his head being hit again. The coldness of the rain sharing his cold sweats. The warm blood on his head sharing his body heat. Dozens of hand shadows of the moaning victims are reaching out from the molded bedroom walls and watered ceiling, reaching for Jonas. The torment didn't stop but grew. The lights flicker on and off, the TV in the living room blares white noise, his home phone rings loudly in his ears. There's a voice on the phone line that's muffled, but from what they say is "Rest for two, we're

Back at the home that used to be nirvana, Kim is still moving things around. She is currently going through boxes of old things. One memory caught her eye as she pulls it out of the box, seeing a picture of her and Jonas's wedding in 1984.

At Bloom-Weather, Jonas is in the kitchen holding onto the picture of him and Eleanor at White Lake. Without a doubt in his mind, he knows his daughter is still alive. No one could tell him otherwise.

Jonas: I'll find you, baby. I promise…

Taking a long lasting look at the photo in high hopes, he goes to his room. Jonas then turns on the light on the nightstand and sits on the edge of the bed as he takes the mysterious note he got that morning. He looks at the note, reading his daughter's name and wanting answers, hoping she's alright, hoping she's okay. With nothing more to see, he puts the note back on the nightstand, turning the light off as he lies down to try and get some sleep.

Chapter 3: Blink of A Dream

Down the quiet halls of Bloom-Weather Apartments, in Jonas's room, he's lying in bed asleep. The hollow walls breathe heavily. His mind plays tricks on him. He can hear the sounds of rusted metal scraping against each other as he hears his own heartbeat. Jonas then hears the faded and distorted moans of the dead victims outside his apartment. His heart starts pounding harder, and he began hearing loud banging outside his door. The ceiling is low and flooded with upside down water dripping onto Jonas and the molded floor. Outside all the windows is nothing but brick walls. He started having flashbacks again of his mother, but she's visually different as her appearance is inhuman. Jonas starts tightening up in fear of his demons. His heart beats faster. Eleanor speaks in his head over and over to the last time they were together.

Eleanor: Daddy!!

Jonas could feel it all over again in replay. He could feel the back of his head being hit again. The coldness of the rain sharing his cold sweats. The warm blood on his head sharing his body heat. Dozens of hand shadows of the moaning victims are reaching out from the molded bedroom walls and watered ceiling, reaching for Jonas. The torment didn't stop but grew. The lights flicker on and off, the TV in the living room blares white noise, his home phone rings loudly in his ears. There's a voice on the phone line that's muffled, but from what they say is "Rest for two, we're watching you." The phrase repeats, and screams become present. Jonas sees room 321 locked with chains blocking the door. He then hears Eleanor's voice again.

Eleanor: Help me, daddy!!! Daddy!!!

Jonas sees himself laughing on the wet sidewalk and bleeding out as he watches his daughter being taken away. He could then hear a voice on the outside call out his name.

...: Jonas! Jonas!

Seconds later, Jonas immediately wakes up from his nightmare seeing he's still in a session with psychologist, Dr. Wilfred.

Dr. Wilfred: Bad dream?... I lost you in a blink...

Jonas: Sorry...

Dr. Wilfred: Are you taking any medication? Jonas?

Jonas: No...

Dr. Wilfred: Okay. That might be something to consider... From what I'm seeing is you're deeply depressed.

Jonas: Depressed?

Jonas didn't know what to think of this session, whether it's a waste of time or a real guidance for his sanity. He sits there on the sofa in the office rubbing his face and trying to keep himself awake.

Dr. Wilfred: Have you been getting any sleep lately?

Jonas: No... It's been hard...

Dr. Wilfred: Okay. Well, do me a favor. Get as much rest as you can. Try and clear your head a little. Come back again tomorrow, and we'll start fresh. Okay? That's it for today.

Jonas: ...Thanks.

Jonas sets foot outside, leaving the counseling center. He takes a deep breath and heads to his car. When he got to his car he calls work. Cyndy picks up on the other end.

Cyndy: Hey. How did it go?

Jonas: I don't know... I was barely there.

Cyndy: What did he say?

Jonas: He told me to get as much rest as I can, and to come back tomorrow.

Cyndy: Are you going to?

Jonas: I don't think I am. I don't feel like it's doing anything for me. I guess I was just doing it for Kim. You know?

Cyndy: Yeah...

Jonas: Do you need me today?

Cyndy: No. We have it covered here. You go on home and try to get you some rest. Do you want me to stop by later?

Jonas: No. That's okay.

Cyndy: Okay... Well, get some sleep.

Jonas: I'll try...

Cyndy: Bye.

Jonas: Bye.

Both of them end the call. Cyndy stands in her office in thought, and Jonas did the same by his car. He then gets in and starts it up to leave.

A few mileages later, Jonas is back at Heaven's Cup. Drinking away his sorrows again, he had a little too much to drink this time. Jonas is then cut off from Hugo's discretion.

Hugo: Alright, Jonas. I'm cutting you off.

Jonas: Fair enough...

He then finishes his last sip in his glass and Hugo hands over a glass of water. Same place by coincidence, Walter walks through the door seeing Jonas at the bar. The old man is tickled by it all.

Walter: Well! Looks like we can have that drink after all!

Jonas: I hate to tell you pal, but I've already been cut off.

Walter: Really?! But it's not even dark out, yet.

Jonas: Yep. It's a shame, but it is what it is. I guess...

Walter: Wow. I knew you were trouble, but not lost.

Jonas: Pfft.

Jonas minds his own and takes a drink of the water.

Walter: Hugo, my friend! I'll take a boop of your superjuice!

Hugo: ...Um?

Walter: Vodka… A small glass, please.

Walter laughs a little to himself from confusing Hugo as he walks off to make his drink.

Walter: So, why are you here this early and already wet?

Jonas: I just wanted some drinks, old man…

Walter: You know? I've already told you my name, but yet you still call me that. I've got more youth in me than you. Of course, I won't go into details about that but- What's your name?

Jonas: Jonas…

Walter then receives his drink, and he quaffed it all down feeling refreshed.

Walter: Ah, I tell ya. Jonas? I drink this stuff like water. I mean, that's what the Russians refer it as.

Jonas: Thanks for the little history lesson. I'm just drinking plain water.

Walter: Hmph. Close enough…

Jonas finishes his water and leaves his payment on the counter. He then gets up to leave; Hugo catches him before he went out the door.

Hugo: Hey. Come on, Jonas. I'm not letting you drive in your condition. Give me your keys.

Jonas: Why don't you just rob me? Here…

He gives Hugo his car keys, protecting him from getting behind the wheel. When he headed out the door, Walter paid and left to catch up. Outside the tavern, Jonas is just a few feet away.

Walter: Hey. Do you need a ride home?

Jonas: No. I'll walk.

Walter: Where do you live?

Jonas: Bloom-Weather. On the other side of town.

Walter: Wow. That's quite a walk to make for being piss drunk.

Jonas: I'm not that bad. I'll manage.

Walter: You know? I live just a few blocks away. Of course, you'd still be walking, but you're welcome to stay at my place, tonight.

Jonas: No thanks.

Walter: You're gonna walk all the way back for your car keys?

Jonas: Look. I'll get a ride from someone. Okay?

Jonas calls work, but didn't get an answer from Cyndy. He leaves her a voicemail and hangs up with options still waiting. Jonas then turns and looks at Walter.

Jonas: You said it was just a few blocks away?

A little bit later, after walking a few blocks, they reached Walter's home. They walk up a few steps to the front door. With Walter making a bunch of noise jangling the keys in the knob, his dog knew he was home. The dog is barking as he unlocked the door.

Walter: That's Bogie. He senses you. Don't worry, he likes company.

After opening the door, they walked inside. Walter turns the light on revealing more of the place. All the walls were filled with décor; old pictures, paintings, a china cabinet that belonged to his mother. Bogie, who's a black Labrador, loves on Walter with excitement, and he then started getting familiar with Jonas, and Jonas shows him his trust petting him a little.

Jonas: Hey, buddy.

Walter: Bogie is old like me. But he's really good at finding things that I never could… Here, have a seat. I'll make some tea.

Jonas sits down on the couch in the living room looking around at all the décor. Bogie follows Walter into the kitchen wagging his tail as Walter put a kettle of tea on the stove to heat up.

After a little bit of time, Walter comes back into the living room with tea. He sits down in a chair in front of Jonas as Bogie lies down on the floor beside him. Walter then gives Jonas the warm tea to help ease his headache.

Jonas: Thanks… I see you're a big fan of antiques.

Walter: Yes. A lot of these are from "Looman Antiques" in western Indiana. That was the last antique shop I've went to ever since Richard died.

Jonas: Is Richard your friend? Or-

Walter: Partner. Or if it were legal, husband.

Jonas: I'm sorry.

Walter: Why are you sorry? That guy was a prick. Hints the name. But I loved him. I still do… Anyways, that grandfather clock was the last thing we bought. He didn't care for it but he knew how much I loved antiques… But enough about me, let's talk about you.

Jonas: What about me? Why does it matter?

Walter: Well, I figured it would be nice to get to know the person I welcomed into my home after them getting drunk enough to not commit sin. Come on. Just be glad I'm not taking advantage of you right now...

Jonas: Um, alright. What do you wanna know?

Walter: Well, first off, something simple. What do you do for a living?

Jonas: I'm a detective. I've been doing it for 12 years now.

Walter: Ah, you must have stories. Untold ones. I'm sure you've seen some horrible things.

Jonas: Yes. They'd give you nightmares. But it comes with the job... However, a lot of bad things are happening here recently...

Walter: I remember reading about the deaths of those children. Such a sad thing to see, it should never happen. The person responsible is such a cruel and disturbed individual, and they're still out there...

Jonas: If you don't mind, I'm going to lay down for a little bit. I have a really bad headache.

Walter: Sure. Would you like me to get you something? Water, a pillow, blanket?-

Jonas: I'm good. Thanks.

Walter: Alright. Well, I'll be down the hall if you need anything. Just holler, I'll hear you. Come on, Bogie.

Walter and his dog go down the long hallway into one of the other rooms to let Jonas rest. He lies back on the couch and closes his eyes. Everything is silent; everything was calm for the brief moment. Until he went back to sleep.

A little bit of time later, and the memories are flooding back into Jonas. The horrors of his past continue to haunt him. The world is nothing, it's gone black, and Jonas is surrounded by darkness. Standing in front of him is an anaglyph version of himself giving an evil glare with a smile. Jonas confronts his shadowed self.

Jonas: Who are you?

N/A: I'm you…

Jonas feared his own self as he could hear Eleanor call out to him from every direction in the darkness. He looks around in a hurry to find his daughter, but his darker self isn't too distracted by it as he watches Jonas act like a fool.

N/A: You don't get it. Do you?... Your daughter is out there waiting for you to come and save her… You told Kim you were going to fix this… And instead, you decide to drown your sorrows to the last drop. Drunk in your hollow town, drinking your spoils down cause you're cheap. You lost everything that completed you… And now you're in limbo thinking you can still save her after all these years… All those other children didn't last. What makes you think her odds are any better?-

Jonas: Shut up!! You don't know anything!

His own evil reflection laughs in his face.

N/A: You're so brash and ignorant… I'm here because you still have your doubts. It's been a while since they've left… **This suffering for receiving is all you will get.**

The words had a heavy faded echo. As Jonas battles with himself, he could hear Eleanor's voice screaming louder for him.

After hearing the sound waves of his daughter's scream, he wakes up gasping for air. The grandfather clock is then chiming at the hour. Jonas sits up on the couch and brings himself to the edge. He rubs his eyes from the tiring stress of his mind. Once the chimes stopped, he could hear the calm tunes of a piano being played down the hall. His head cleared for a bit from the music bringing him remembrance of a good memory from his past.

After sitting around for a little while, Jonas gets up from the couch and follows the sound down the hall. Walking down the hallway he stops at one of the middle rooms seeing Walter playing on an old piano. Jonas is then an audience for Walter with Bogie at the old man's side as he gently presses the keys, playing notes in an elegant manner. Jonas's eyes begin to water a little appearing red with a vague smile as he goes way back, missing the times he had. He continues to stand at the doorway to listen, and Walter finishes up the song in silence.

Jonas: ...That was really nice.

Walter: My mother would always play that piece when I was a little boy...

Jonas: Kim used to play the piano... We met at a friend's party. While everybody else was drinking, talking, and just having a good time, she was sitting in the living room playing music… I'll never forget that day.

Walter: She sounds like a wonderful lady.

Jonas: She is.

Walter: I'd like to meet her someday. Are you two still together?

Jonas: No… We got divorced 6 years ago.

Walter: I'm sorry… I didn't mean to-

Jonas: It's okay, Walter… Last time I spoke with her, she thought that I needed to get help… I tried talking to a psychologist, but I don't think that'll help me…

Walter: I'm not a fan of psychologists or psychiatrists. I think they're all pill-pushers for your money… That's a shame… Other than your poor drinking habits, you're a fine young man…

Jonas: Listen. I wanna say thank you again for letting me stay here tonight.

Walter: Now, don't be getting all melancholy on me. That's no fun. You're a guest, you're a friend, and there's no thanks necessary. Now, are you hungry for food?

Jonas: Yes. I could eat.

Walter: Good. 'Cause I'm starving. I didn't want to be rude. That was thoughtful of me wasn't it?... You don't have to answer that.

Walter walks out of the room past Jonas, laughing at himself. Jonas smirks with troubling thoughts still placed at the back of his head feeling that his time is being wasted from his own faults.

After the night at Walter's home, it's the next morning. Jonas starts to wake up back on the couch from the hourly chime of the grandfather clock. He sits up trying to fully get himself up as the sounds and smells of sizzling bacon are being made. Shortly then, Jonas walks into the kitchen seeing Walter finishing up a small breakfast on the stove. Walter then places the cooked eggs from the pan onto his plate that was ready on the table.

Walter: I hope you like your eggs over easy.

Jonas: Yes, I do.

Walter: Good, because that's the only way that I make them.

Walter chuckles a little by his honesty.

Walter: I'm sorry. I'll shut up. Richard wouldn't have laughed either... He was a really good cook, when he wanted to cook.

Jonas: Well, this is great. Thank you.

Walter: Wait 'til you have some of my waffles.

After eating a little bit, Jonas excuses himself from the table.

Jonas: I'm gonna make a call. Excuse me.

He then leaves the kitchen to call for a ride. Making the call, he gets an answer.

Jonas: Hey... I'm gonna need a ride.

A little bit later, after breakfast and making a phone call, Jonas's ride pulls up. Walter is then walking him to the door.

Walter: You know. I could've given you a ride to your car.

Jonas: I'm not gonna go get my car. I'll get it later today. I'm just gonna go straight to the station... Once again, Walter, thank you for letting me stay here last night.

Walter: I enjoyed your company. You're welcome here anytime, Jonas... I hope you don't hesitate to come back...

Jonas: Take care, Walter.

Without further conversation, Jonas walks down the steps towards his ride as Walter closes the door. He gets inside Zach's car, and they leave Walter's place. Heading through to the other side of the town, Aqua Heights is nothing but fog from the streams underground and the cool air. On the road Zach starts making conversation.

Zach: So who was that back there?

Jonas: A friend…

Zach: Hmph… So uh, things were a little tense between you and me back at the station when you left a few days ago. Are you ready to talk about it now? I need to know what's going on, Jonas.

Jonas keeps to himself for a little longer trying to avoid the topic. Zach becomes a little impatient.

Zach: Yeah. That's fine. I get it… We've been partners for 8 years, Jonas. I am your friend in and outside of work. You can trust me… Just know if you don't tell me what's going on, then I can't help you.

After their very short talk, they pull up at the station. Before Zach got out of the car, Jonas stops him.

Jonas: Wait… Close the door.

Zach then closes his door and sits back to listen to Jonas open up the truth.

Jonas: ... You know those cases we opened back up? When I woke up the next morning, I got a message that had a lily flower and my daughter's name on it...

Zach: ...Geezus...

Jonas: I don't know why now... But I think she's still alive... And I have to find the son-of-a-bitch that's doing this...

Zach: ...Okay. I'm with you... I'm with you on this, Jonas...

Jonas: Thank you...

After Jonas filled Zach in on what's been going on, they exit the car and head inside the station. They make themselves some coffee to help them focus on their tasks before separating their work.

Zach: I'm going to look at a few older files and see if there's something we've missed. Maybe find more connections between this and the other cases.

Jonas: Alright. I'll let Cyndy know.

As Zach starts to head the other way, he stops to tell Jonas something.

Zach: Jonas… If she's alive, we'll find her…

Zach then continues down the main hall to go search for more connections. Jonas kept silent in hoping that he would find his daughter alive. He then heads in the opposite direction to find Cyndy.

Once Jonas made it to Cyndy's office they discuss their matters.

Jonas: Hey, Cyndy. I told Zach about Eleanor… He wants to help too. Him and I are gonna look back at the files of the older cases and see if we can find more connections.

Cyndy: That's good. We'll need all the help we can get… But Jonas… I know this is personal for you, and I just want to know if you should even be taking part in this.

Jonas: Yes, I should! This is my daughter!

Cyndy: I just need you to remember how these things can be.

Jonas: Cyndy. You don't need to worry about me.

Cyndy: I just care, Jonas.

Jonas: Then let me do this... I know you'd want to do the same...

Jonas made his point clear to Cyndy that he isn't going to step away from this case. Without further discussions, he leaves her office. She takes a deep breath in concern for Jonas as he feels a little upset from her suggestion. Jonas then sits at his desk with some coffee and old case files to search through.

After a long day, Jonas is still sitting at his desk with little sense of progress and frustration. He had all sorts of notes written down, addresses circled, names underlined, etc. Most of what he gathered was crossed out from the little bit of information that he had. He stops to keep himself from getting lost in his own madness. Jonas then gathers his notes and files, and packs up for the day. Before leaving, he stops by Cyndy's office to wish her a good night.

Jonas: Hey. I'll see you tomorrow.

Cyndy: Alright. I'll see you then...

Jonas: ...I'm sorry, about earlier today... It's just that... I can't step away from this...

Cyndy: I know...

Jonas: Have a good night, Cyndy.

Cyndy: Good night.

While Cyndy finishes up paperwork in her office, Jonas starts heading for the doors. On his way down the hall he passes up Zach.

Zach: I haven't found much so far. Any luck on your end?

Jonas: No. I just got a few list of names but nothing to go on...

Zach: I knew this wasn't going to be easy.

Jonas: It never is... I'm headed home. We'll start back up in the morning.

Zach: Alright. I'll take another gander at these files tonight. I'll let you know what I find. Oh, and I had a tow truck bring your car, earlier. You don't owe me anything; it's already been taken care of. Here's your keys.

Jonas: Thank you, Zach.

Zach: Hey. We're a team. This time, we're gonna close this case the right way. Drive safe.

Jonas: You too.

Zach and Jonas leave the building and part ways to their vehicles. They both drive in opposite directions from the parking lot, headed home. Driving on the road late at night, Jonas is behind the wheel thinking on whether or not he'd find a lead to his daughter. His mind is twisting him more and more as he grips the wheel to focus.

A little later back at the station, Cyndy is still alone in her office. She then starts feeling sick to her stomach and in thought of Jonas's safety. Cyndy hunches over her desk feeling nauseous. Moments later, she quickly grabs the small trashcan beside her, puking a little from all she has concerning her. Feeling a little weak from her body she thinks to herself. Cyndy looks at her purse knowing what she had.

After a little while of driving, Jonas is then home. He unlocks the door and walks inside his apartment. Jonas felt this long day drag with him, and he feels heavily disappointed that he found no other answers that would bring him closer to finding his daughter. He hangs up his coat, tosses his keys onto the kitchen counter, and sits down on the couch in exhaustion as he could hear his neighbors next door arguing loudly again about something. Ignoring everything else around him, Jonas turns on the TV for a little bit as he feels his failure all together in front of the bright screen.

Back at the station, Cyndy is in the women's restroom feeling nervous about herself as she finishes taking a pregnancy test. She could feel herself shaking and having trouble breathing as she waited for the results. After waiting for a few minutes, she looks at the stick and sees that the results are positive. Cyndy is in shock with mixed tears of joy and fear of not knowing what she was going to do for this child of hers. She then thinks about Jonas, not knowing what she'll say to him as she sits there quietly in the cold stall.

A little later after an hour or so, Jonas was asleep in front of the TV. He then manages to wake back up feeling how tired he is. He grabs the remote and turns off the TV, and he leaves the living room to go to bed. Standing by the nightstand and his bed, he's checking his Taurus Tracker .44 MAG revolver, looking to make sure it was loaded as he twists the cartridge a little hearing its clicks. He then puts the gun down on the nightstand along with his cell phone and he crawls into bed. Jonas is lying there for a moment, staring at the ceiling fan with high hopes in the dark. With nothing else to do, he turns off the lamp light to get some sleep.

Chapter 4: Neighboring Waters

Early the next morning around 5, Jonas is waking up from a phone call on his cell. He looks at the name seeing it is Zach. He then answers the phone.

Jonas: Hello?

Zach: Hey. I'm sorry to call you at this hour, but I'm just now thinking of this. Those two girls from the other cases. April and Eirene? They were both found near water… You last saw your daughter at Blue Creek Park. Right?

Jonas has a quick flashback of him losing his daughter again. He was quiet for a moment but then speaks.

Jonas: Yeah.

Zach: Blue Creek is right next to Baleen River… You think there might be something there?

Jonas: We're about to find out. I'm gonna get ready, then I'll meet you at your place. I'll see you in an hour.

Zach: Alright.

Jonas hangs up and gets out of his bed and starts getting ready early for the day. He puts on some old work boots, grabs his gun from the nightstand placing it in his small of back holster. Jonas then grabs his phone and takes his coat and keys on the way out the door.

A couple hours later, it is brighter outside. Another morning that is slightly foggy with quiet chills from the calm air. Jonas and Zach are pulling up in the parking lot of Blue Creek Park down by the riverside away from town. They both get out of the car to look around. No one else is in sight. It all feels disturbing to Jonas revisiting this place as he looks around him with distractions in his head.

Zach: Hey. – Hey. Stay focused and let's see what we can find.

Jonas: Yeah. Okay...

Jonas clears up his head as him and Zach start looking around the area. They could hear the birds chirping in the sky and the wind blowing from the water flow. Jonas starts walking downhill passing some of the dark trees towards the shore of the river. Closer down the wet slope, Jonas finds something.

Jonas: Over here.

Zach walks over to Jonas pointing out some white flower petals embedded in mud leading down to the river. They look at each other knowing there is more to find, and they head further down. Following the trail of petals, they reach the shore. The sound of the river is louder in the cold air as they look around for more signs left by the suspect. Looking around closely at their surroundings they notice the big rotted tree at the end of the small beachside lying partially in the shallow part of the river. Jonas then begins to see something else out of the ordinary. Getting closer to the tree and past some brushes of twigs is a rope tied on one of the thick branches. They see the rope leading into water of the river with no slack left. Jonas then grabs the rope and starts to pull, and as he pulls he can feel something heavy on the other end.

After pulling more and more of the rope, they see something coming around the other side of the tree and poking out of the water around some lotuses. Jonas starts pulling harder and harder for them to get a closer look. It didn't take long for them to know that Jonas was pulling out a dead body from the river. Seeing the corpse on shore, the skin is badly wrinkled, the body is wearing multiple green floaties with a tight noose around their neck and some old puncture wounds. After seeing the nasty sight, it was time to inform others.

Jonas: Go ahead and call this in. I'm calling Cyndy.

A little bit later, other investigators and authorities are at the scene. More evidence is carefully being collected. Cyndy's looking at the victim's ID from their wallet reading information on it.

Cyndy: This is Ronnie Wallace. He's retired; he used to be a landlord.

Jonas: … He used to own Bloom-Weather Apartments. Back when me and my mother lived there…

Zach: The flower petals were left here on purpose. I think he wanted us to find this.

Cyndy: The flower was torn apart this time. I'm not sure if that means something… But his targets are children. Why would he change that?

Jonas: … I don't know…

Jonas walks back over to Ronnie's corpse examining it. When he sees the floaties he reads "Aberdeen Watermill" as a part of its labeled property.

Jonas: "Aberdeen Watermill..." Do you know where that is?

Zach: Yeah. That's upriver. It's about 4 miles out.

Jonas: Alright. That's where we're heading.

Cyndy: I'll follow you up there.

Jonas: Alright. Well, I'm ready now.

The three of them leave the crime scene at Baleen River and they get in their vehicles to head upriver. They're then driving out in the countryside on the long open road that's covered in rainbows of graffiti and surrounded by fall-winter trees in the hills of the mountain.

About 4 miles later, they reach the old watermill. A large white wooded building out in the woods by the river. They pull their cars up beside each other out front and they step out onto the wet and dry leaves. The wind would blow occasionally, blowing some leaves and small branches around. Other than the wind, it's pretty quiet. The watermill doesn't look like it's been operated for a long time, but clearly shows someone lives there. The three of them walk up on the big porch to the main door. Jonas knocks on the door, but there's no response. He knocks again as Cyndy tries peeking through the drapes in the front windows.

After waiting longer than a minute, there still is no response. This place gave nothing but a strange and creepy feeling. They all look at each other in suspicion of the whole setting and no one coming to the door.

Cyndy: I'll head around back. See if I can find another way in.

Zach: I'll come with you.

Cyndy: It's okay, Zach. I can handle myself. Just keep your eyes and ears open. Something isn't right, here.

Jonas: Yeah. Be careful.

Cyndy: You too.

Cyndy then pulls out her gun and heads around on the wraparound porch looking for another way inside. Jonas and Zach pull out their guns as they manage to open the front door since it was unlocked. The door opens slowly and creaks quietly with the wind blowing inside, and the two them enter with caution. Signs of the old building showed from the worn floorboards creaking from their footsteps. They look around for anything that may connect more to their case as their time is ticking.

Meanwhile, Cyndy finds another door around the backside. She walks into a part of the interior with old giant gearwheels and pumps along with some hollow plastic mannequins that were stored away and are covered in cobwebs and dust. Cyndy then makes her way into the main part of the building finding herself in another room. This room wasn't necessarily a bedroom, but it has a mattress. Beside it is a plate of food that has been eaten off of. Cyndy hovers her hand over the food feeling a little bit of heat rising. She then knew that whoever is living here is close by. Becoming more alert and keeping her eyes open she sees something on the other side of the room on an old chest box. She walks over to it to get a closer look and sees that it's a blue elephant stuffed animal. It looks a little old but familiar, and that she recognizes it from somewhere. There's a small draft of air that blows by her. When she turns around, she's attacked by a swinging blow to her stomach from a baseball bat. She immediately falls down to the floor with the wind knocked out of her. She struggles to breathe and talk as she barely lifts up from the floor in deep pain.

Cyndy: N-N-no!

She coughs and gasps as she felt upset with shocking pain and worry from being pregnant. Before she had a chance to shoot, the middle aged man kicks her upside the head and she is knocked out cold. Before finishing her off, the man knew there were others inside. He takes Cyndy's gun to make things easier and walks away to get rid of the others.

In the same moment, Jonas and Zach are looking deeper and find something more disturbing.

Zach: What the hell?...

On one of the walls is an old community board with missing posters of children, including the ones that were found dead, along with some newspaper articles about the murders. Things became more frightening and alarming to Jonas when he sees the missing poster of his daughter tacked to the board with the others.

Jonas: I gotta find her...

Zach: Where's Cyndy? She needs to see this.

Zach then starts looking for Cyndy and calling out for her.

Zach: Cyndy?

No response came from Cyndy. A red flag is up, Zach and Jonas both raise up their guns in ready. Cyndy is still lying down on the cold hardwood floor in a daze with a bloody nose. She could barely move at this moment. Cyndy then starts reaching for her other gun that she had hidden on her ankle.

At this point, Zach and Jonas are proceeding further with caution. Zach calls out for Cyndy again.

Zach: Cyndy?

There's still no response from her as they start moving into another part of the house. Walking around one of the corners is a surprise of a baseball bat being swung. Zach is hit in his arms making him grunt loudly as he's disarmed of his firearm. The gun slides across the floor and Zach quickly tries throwing a punch. The man stops him at first but Zach is quick to throw his other fist. Hitting the man hard a few times, he hits even harder. Weakening Zach, the man knees him down to the floor. Jonas quickly comes around with his gun aiming at him as he yells.

Jonas: FREEZE!

The suspect is caught by surprise and quickly runs off into another room dropping the bat as Jonas fires his gun. He frantically empties a few bullets out of his gun hitting nothing but the walls. Jonas keeps his gun up and eyes open as it goes quiet again. He looks over at Zach seeing him hurt on the floorboard.

Jonas: You alright?!

Zach: Yeah!

Zach remains down as Jonas looks swiftly between the rooms that connect. Letting his guard down for a second he's then jumped by the suspect. The surprise and force of his weight and appearance causes Jonas to fire another shot into the floor. The suspect overpowers Jonas and pins him up roughly against the wall strangling him. While Jonas is trying to fight back, Zach grabs an old wooden chair and breaks it across the man's back. The suspect lets go of Jonas, letting him gasp for air as he grabs Zach and throws him across the table in the room. He then pulls out the gun he took from Cyndy and aims it at Jonas who's breathless and is staring at the barrel. As Zach is lying on the floor he sees his gun. The bad man gives an evil smile at Jonas as he's about to win the fight. He pulls the trigger, firing nothing but the sound of a click. The gun was a decoy catching the suspect off guard. The man then quickly hovers over Jonas about to beat him bloody with the gun as Zach retrieved his and is aiming at the man. Before Zach got in a shot, Cyndy beat him to it as she fired a few rounds into the guy, putting him down. She stood at the doorway holding her stomach, wounded and weary. The hot smoke is slowly coming out of the barrel of her gun as she lowers it back down knowing that the fight is over.

A little bit later after their confrontation, other responders are there at the scene. All the different department branches are there for the excitement. Criminalists' and other techs are entering the house as their dead suspect is being rolled out on a stretcher in a body bag. Cyndy is sitting in the back of an ambulance getting a little bit of medical attention. She is motionless and looked a little drained from today. Jonas walks over to check on her.

Jonas: How are you holding up?

Cyndy: I should be asking you that.

Jonas: …I was really hoping we'd find her…

Cyndy: I know…

They both see the body being loaded up in the back of another ambulance. Neither one shows any emotion towards it. However, Jonas could see that Cyndy's mind is somewhere else.

Jonas: Are you bothered by it?

Cyndy: That's not what's bothering me…

Cyndy gets up and starts walking away to leave.

Cyndy: I'm gonna go…

Jonas: Do you want some company?

Cyndy: No. No. I want to be left alone. Thanks…

Cyndy didn't say another word nor did she look back as Jonas watches her walk away. When she got in her car and left, Zach is walking up.

Zach: Where is she going?

Jonas: I don't know.

Zach: Is she okay?

Jonas: Probably not.

Zach: ...Hey, I uh- saw this in another room and thought that you might want it...

Zach shows Jonas the blue elephant that belonged to his daughter. Jonas's eyes open wide and become a little glassy from the sight of it as he slowly clinches onto the stuffed animal. This is the closest he's felt to his daughter in a long time, and it kills him even more inside. He closes his eyes taking it all in with a deep breath.

Jonas: Where the hell is she, Zach?

Zach: I don't know...

Jonas: Is this supposed to be his trophy?! I just want my daughter back!

Zach: We don't need to talk about this right now. You already got a lot on your mind-

Jonas: I know what I got!

Zach: ...We'll talk about this, later. Alright?

Jonas looks at Zach without a word to say, and he looks away as he feels frustrated with the endless loops and no resolutions.

Later after Aberdeen, Jonas and Zach make it back to the station. Rain is coming down heavily. As they're sitting in the parking lot, Zach starts opening his door.

Jonas: Zach... I'm not in the wrong here... This doesn't add up. That guy isn't the one who took Eleanor... He had some dark secrets. But it's not the guy...

Zach: Are you saying he was set up?

Jonas: I'm saying this is a misguide. Not all the evidence is there. As much as I wish it was. He wouldn't make it this easy, and he wouldn't lead us right to him like that. This guy was only after children, he wanted to keep himself low profile...

Zach: Look, we all had a hell of a day. We need to clear our heads-

Jonas: You had a hell of a day?!! Every day my life is hell! This is my daughter! And I will not stop until I find her! I am clearheaded!

Zach: I want to find her too, Jonas! Me and Cyndy! You can't do this alone! Every day, every second that goes by, this case gets colder!... Your best chance in finding your daughter is by letting us help you... We just need to find our answers before we go running in the dark...

Zach then reopens his door into the pouring rain.

Zach: Get some rest, if you can.

With no response to give, Zach shuts the door as Jonas is frozen still with his hands gripping the wheel tightly as he's slowly losing his mind from all the rage.

Later on, Jonas is back at Bloom-Weather. Walking down the hallway a little soaked, he could hear how hard the rain is coming down. Walking further down, that isn't the only thing he could hear. His neighbors are arguing again, but it sounds worse. Jonas is standing at the door to his apartment as he listens to the verbal abuse coming from a man yelling at a helpless woman who yelled back with the sound of tears. Jonas could then hear some furniture being flipped over as the woman cries. He had enough of the bullshit he was hearing and he knocks loudly on their door. It got quiet and the door opens with the woman standing there to answer. She quickly started wiping up her tears as she stood in the dim light of her hall.

Jonas: Iris? Is everything alright? I could hear you two down the hallway.

Iris: I'm sorry, Jonas. Yes. Everything's fine.

Jonas: You can tell me anything. You know that. Right?

Iris: Yeah...

Jonas knew that she was hiding her fears and bigger problems as she's keeping shy in the dark. They both heard the man in the back impatiently wondering what was taking so long. Jonas presses further.

Jonas: Iris. Can you step outside for a minute?

Iris: ...S-sure... I'm stepping out for a sec!

Iris then steps out into the hallway leaving the door cracked behind her. She spoke quietly and anxiously with her arms crossed, not making eye contact. Her short black hair is covering most of her face.

Iris: What do you want?

Jonas: I wanna know that you're truly okay.

Iris: I'm fine…

Jonas: Look at me.

Iris hesitates, but she turns to him and is acting like everything is fine even though she couldn't hide her cut lip or dark bruises on her face once she showed him. The sight of Iris's abuse struck Jonas with hurt and more anger.

Iris: I'm fine. Nothing's broken… He was a little high when it happened. Okay?

Jonas: Dammit! It's not okay, Iris! It's gotten worse ever since he came back… What about your little boy? What does he think seeing you, his mother covered in bruises by his father?

Iris: He's staying at my mom's right now. I try not to have him around when he's like this... Please... He just got out...

Jonas: Iris. I need to talk to him.

Iris: The drugs were mine, Jonas. He got high because of me.

Jonas: I don't give a shit that he was high.

Before she could speak any more, her boyfriend is at the door.

Iris: Kess. It's okay, we were just talking-

Kess: About what?! Get inside! Do I gotta tell you twice?!

Iris didn't argue, and she does as he says. Kess and Jonas look dead at each other with their differences and grudges against one another.

Jonas: Kessinger. You and I need to talk.

Kess: We don't got fucking nothing to talk about!

Kess then shuts the door. Jonas stands there with boiling anger, hearing Iris apologize over and over, and begging until she is slapped hard. Jonas didn't think and just opens up the door, walking in seeing Iris on the tile floor of the kitchen sitting up against the cabinets with tears rolling down her cheeks. Kess is standing at the entry way between the kitchen and the living room.

Jonas: Don't lay another hand on her!

Kess: What the hell are you doing?!! Mind your own fucking business!!

As Jonas is approaching, Kess quickly throws a punch. Jonas stops the throw midway and throws back a punch to his stomach and face knocking him back against the wall. Kess got angrier and he charges at Jonas, tackling him through a glass table and onto the floor with the shattered glass.

Iris: Kess!! Kess!! Stop!!

Iris is hitting on Kess's back trying to stop him as he's choking Jonas. Kess shoves Iris back giving Jonas an opening, and he knocks him in the jaw and off the top of him. Being hit again and adding on to his rage, Kess pulls out a gun tucked in the back of his pants. Jonas quickly reacts, kicking Kess's arm away from aiming as he loses his balance falling back to the floor. When Kess tries turning back around, Jonas clocks him in the face again. Jonas is then on top of Kess on his backside kicking the gun away from his reach. He then starts putting him in handcuffs. He makes them tighter and tighter on his wrists causing him to grunt from discomfort.

Jonas: I don't give a damn if these cut off your blood circulation… You assaulted an officer, asshole… Not only that. I got you for a stolen firearm. And not to mention what you've been doing to Iris and your son… They're gonna be glad to have you back in prison after hearing about the abuse you gave to them.

Jonas then roughly pulls Kess off the living room floor. He has a good grip on his shirt, and is not being gentle leading him out of the apartment. On his way out, he stops and looks at Iris who looks broken and tired of her struggles in life. She stares back at Jonas with her fresh bruises and watered glassy eyes. Her soft hopeless stare shattered a small piece of Jonas. Not a moment later, he then quickly went on his way out, taking Kess with him.

Later, the rain is still coming down hard as Jonas is waiting outside with Kess. A few seconds later, a cop car pulls up to them. The officer steps out and takes Kess off of Jonas's hands.

Jonas: Hey. He was using, so you're gonna want be sure to read him his Miranda rights again. Alright? Thank you.

The officer starts escorting Kess to the back of the car in the pouring rain. Once they left, Jonas heads back inside.

Three floors later, Jonas is walking back to his apartment. On the way there, he sees Iris standing outside her door with tears and anxiety. Her and Jonas look at each other as she's shook up. Before opening the door, Jonas didn't want to leave her worried.

Jonas: I'll pay for the damages and get you a new table... I'm— I'm not sorry for what I did, Iris... I'm sorry for not doing something sooner. But I'll make sure that he won't hurt you and your son anymore... You'll be able to see your son again... Before you do though, you should get yourself clean...

Iris: I will... Thank you...

Jonas unlocks his door and starts to step inside, but then Iris spoke.

Iris: I'm sorry about your daughter...

Jonas is standing still in the doorway looking into his apartment in silence. He then looks at Iris with attention, hiding his sadness deeply inside of him.

Jonas: Thanks… Take better care of yourself, Iris…

Iris: You too…

Without saying more, Iris watches Jonas enter his apartment. Once he closed his door she too goes back to her apartment, going their separate ways. An act of oneself, a good deed was done today. Justified, it satisfied a little for the lows from earlier of today. Jonas walks down the hallway rubbing his sore neck from the fight. He walks in the kitchen and makes a small glass of ice. His knuckles are bruised red from the blunt trauma as he holds the small glass, pouring some aged scotch.

Jonas: Here's to you, Walter.

Jonas takes a drink and puts the empty glass of ice aside. He then sits down on the couch in the living room exhausted and stares off in space. Sitting in the silent room moments later, he gets a text from Zach. It was more info for Jonas. The text said "The guy we took down today was Barney Cobain." Jonas sits there for a moment, and he then gets up to grab his coat. Once he was ready to head out, he grabs his keys and leaves his apartment again to go back down to the station.

Meanwhile, Iris is in her apartment 318. She had made herself some hot tea in a big cup to give her warmth and comfort in her gloomy place. Iris walks into the living room looking at the broken table with shatters of glass on the floor. She sits down in a recliner sipping on her tea as she thinks to herself. With a little bit of time passing by, she looks at the nightstand next to her seeing some of the used heroin along with a syringe, a spoon, and a lighter. All of it shining under the lamp in a glimpse of her old paradise. She stares at it with temptation until she gave in. Iris takes some of the heroin and boils it in the spoon with the lighter until it was liquid. She then draws it up in the syringe for a dose. When it was ready for use, she took an elastic band to do the twist around her arm, looking for a vein to shoot. Iris is having a fit searching desperately for a vein, and when she finally found one she had the needle ready. She then stops herself and is sweating bullets with hesitation of her addiction as she looks at her arm showing marks from previous injections. After looking at the marks, she looks at the hard drug she was about to inject into her body again, and she then thought of her son. Iris closes her eyes feeling release and shame, and she lays down the syringe not taking the heroin. She then grabs a large thick trash bag and starts cleaning up the mess of glass that was on her floor. Putting all of the broken glass in the bag as she also puts the drugs and needle in with it. Iris leaves her apartment to take out the trash. A few moments later, she makes it out to the dumpster in the pouring rain. Iris tosses the trash and a part of her rough life away. When Iris made it back to her apartment, she pulls out an older picture of her and her son from the drawer of the nightstand. She sets the picture up under the light. The good memories brought her tears and a sad smile, and she knew this is a step towards getting better for her son.

In the intervening time period, Jonas pulls up at the station at night. Once he made his way inside and to the main offices, he went into the storage room. Searching through dusty filing cabinets, looking through old reports and criminal records, he finds Barney Cobain's file in the old list of names that were kept away.

BARNEY'S FILE:

Age: 57

Weight: 216lbs

Height: 75"

Hair Color: Light Brown

Looking deeper in his file, Jonas finds an article about Barney's arrest back in 1980. The title read "Man Arrested for Ten Missing Children." Reading further down it mentions 39 yr old Barney Cobain was escorted out of "Alchemilla Orphanage" by law enforcement at 6am on a Sunday morning and has been taken into custody for questioning and possible charges. "No further information has been given at this time" is the last reading line of the short article. Barney's folder was thick, so Jonas knows there's more information about him, but he closes it up for now and takes it with him.

During that time somewhere else, at the bar, Hugo is cleaning out the empty glasses as he sees the news on the TV mentioning Barney's death report from earlier that day.

After the rain had stopped, while going for a walk down the street alone that night, Iris sees the news playing on multiple screens of advertised TVs sitting behind a big glass window of a store.

Concurrently, Kim is sitting alone in the living room watching the news until she shut it off with nothing left to warm her in her sad life.

Meanwhile, at Walter's home, Walter is watching the same channel with the news on his TV. Collected photos of Barney's old whereabouts and his setups of the missing children posters were displayed on the screen. It all is an upsetting thing for Walter to see as he didn't want to watch anymore.

Around the same time at Zach's place, Zach is sitting at his kitchen table drunk by the big bottle of booze sitting in front of him. He looks at some pictures that he has with the faces of all the missing children that were on the missing posters, now scattered on the table in front of him. Feeling like the empty bottle, he hides his face in his arms and crying hard with suffering.

Another life with lost hope, Cyndy is at the hospital. She's sitting in a room having an ultrasound. Cyndy's emotions are a void as she sits there patiently listening for a heartbeat. The longer she sat there the more the feeling started coming back. With a heartbeat that's not there anymore, a tear rolled down her face from her blinking eyes.

Back again at Jonas's apartment, he sits the folder with Barney's name on it aside. He turns on the TV to see what was being showed to the rest of the town. Jonas felt nothing but annoyance from it. He then pulls the folder over to him and opens it up to do some work.

Chapter 5: The Door of Alchemilla

Early the next morning, Jonas is up and getting ready for work. Files are scattered all across his coffee table from last night. He's called Zach multiple times and hasn't gotten a call back. Jonas tried Cyndy's cell multiple times, and he didn't hear from her either but her voicemail.

Jonas: Hey. Cyndy. It's Jonas. I tried calling Zach's cell, but I haven't heard from him yet. I just wanted to let you know that I found some old files on Barney from the watermill house that were hidden away at the station. I've been looking through it, and I found some old articles that mention him being an employee at "Alchemilla Orphanage." I'm hoping to find some answers there… I hope you're doing okay. Just call me when you can. Get some sleep. Okay? Bye.

Jonas hangs up the phone and starts to head out the door. When Jonas made it to his car, his phone started ringing. It's Zach returning his calls.

Jonas: Hey. I tried calling you.

Zach: I know. I'm sorry. I was up late last night. What did you need?

Jonas: I found some old files of that guy Barney at the station last night.

Zach: What else did you find?

Jonas: Some old newspaper articles about his arrest at "Alchemilla Orphanage" when some children from there went missing back in 1980.

Zach: Alchemilla?

Jonas: You know the place?

Zach: Yeah. I've heard of it. It's not an orphanage anymore though.

Jonas: He used to be an employee there. I'm headed there to see what else I can find.

Zach: Alright. I'm looking over a few things here.

Jonas: See if you can get in contact with anyone who used to be staff members there. Therapists, directors, anybody that worked there during the time those kids went missing.

Zach: Alright. I'm on it.

After their call ended, Jonas is on his way to the old orphanage. He looks at the blue elephant that's a little dirty and worn. Something ran by him, and he needed to make a stop at his friend, Walter.

A little bit later, Jonas pulls in front of Walter's home. He gets out of his car and walks up to the front door. After knocking and calling his name a few times, he answers.

Walter: Hey! Look who it is.

Jonas: Hey Walter. I've got a favor to ask.

Walter: Okay… What's the favor?

Jonas: Do you mind if I take Bogie for a little bit? I need him to help me find what I'm looking for.

Walter: ...Jonas. As much as I'd like to help, I don't feel comfortable with that. Bogie is really old. He has the nose of a bloodhound, but he's not a K9. I'm sorry.

Jonas: Okay...

Walter then sees the stuffed animal in Jonas's hand. While Jonas is still standing at the door, Bogie makes his way from the living room to him.

Walter: Bogie?! Get back! Bogie!

Bogie smells the stuffed animal in Jonas's hand. Jonas didn't know what it meant, but he knew the dog is getting a strong scent off of it. Bogie then started to bark and growl at the scent from the stuffed animal.

Walter: Bogie! Go!

The dog backed off and listened. Walter looked back at Jonas, knowing something was up with that stuffed animal, and Jonas could see it.

Jonas: What is it?

Walter: ...Nothing good... Whatever it was, it bothered him...

Jonas: ...Thank you for your time. I'm sorry for causing a problem... Take care...

Walter closes the door and Jonas turns away. He knows that nothing good came from the scent. Jonas had a little bit a worry and anxiety, but he keeps it under control for now. He heads back to his car and gets inside, tossing the stuffed animal aside. Jonas sits in the driver seat and looks over at the blue elephant in the passenger seat. He got curious, and thought about what Walter said before, about Bogie being good at finding things. Jonas then grabs the blue elephant and feels around, examining it closely. He could feel something hard inside of it. Jonas then easily manages to tear a little opening in the back of it to see what was.

After digging a little bit, he pulls out what was hidden inside. It's an old key. Jonas looked confused, and he knew that this key wasn't there before. Without wasting any more time, he holds onto it. Jonas then starts the car, and gets back on the road to go to Alchemilla.

Later on this same day, Jonas is still on the road. The fog and steam has risen and thickened more as he got closer to Alchemilla. Further out in the open woods, up the mountain away from town, he made it to the orphanage. It's old, white and grey, wood and stone walls, and its tall stained windows are its features from the outside. The building looks like a combination of a church and a lighthouse by its old structure. Jonas pulls in the gravel lot just below it. As he's sitting in the car, his radio was nothing but static muffling in and out. He then steps outside of the car, into the dull whiteness that's in the air. Suddenly the loud ringing of church bells made its presence, scaring some ravens from the roof and trees. Jonas then makes his way up a long set of stairs that led uphill to the building, passing a sign that read "Alchemilla Church" along the way. When he reached the top and stood in front of the big dark wooded doors, he knocks.

A few moments later, with no one there to answer, Jonas starts to open the door and walks inside. Now in the entrance room, there's another set of doors. He opens the second set of doors leading him into the main part of the church. The air is silent. A few candles are lit around the empty room. Jonas walks down the middle aisle, passing the long rows of benches, looking around at all the different showings of religions. On one of the walls, there's some old woodwork that showed going around and filled in what used to be a doorway. Jonas could hear his own footsteps echoing inside the old church until someone spoke in his presence, catching him by surprise.

...: Hello… Sorry. I didn't mean to startle you… I'm Father Michael. How can I help you, son?

Jonas: Hello. Father. I'm with the police. I came here looking for answers.

Father Michael: What answers are you looking for?

Jonas: Something that'll tell me more about Barney Cobain.

Father Michael didn't speak once he heard the name, but he felt a dark presence by his mentioning.

Jonas: Do you remember him?

Father Michael: Yes. I remember him since he was a little boy… It's sad how his life was.

Jonas: Do you know anyone else in his family that might be able to answer some questions?

Father Michael: Barney never had a family. He was an orphan here all his life…

Jonas: There's never been any mentions of his real parents or anyone?

Father Michael: No. He was abandoned at birth, and left to die. Someone said they found him in a boiler room at Lincoln High School. That school's not there anymore... But after he was at the hospital for a few weeks, he was brought here.

Jonas: Did he ever go anywhere when he was older? Like in town or somewhere he liked to visit often?

Father Michael: Well, none of the children were allowed to leave here without supervision. But he did like going to the lake that's down the hill, past the trees.

Jonas: Barney liked being around water?

Father Michael: Yes. I'd say so. He was the janitor here too.

Jonas: Did Barney like being around the other children when he was younger?

Father Michael: Well, from what I remember, he didn't really talk much to the other kids. He was the quiet one of the bunch. But he never caused problems with the others... I know old news may not show that now, but... No one here was ever suspicious of him.

Jonas: Well, when he was being held for a little while, they couldn't find anything against him that held him responsible for those missing children. They eventually ended up having to let him go... Things were different back then...

Father Michael: Yeah. We still had one child with us when they took Barney into custody. His name was "Isaac Rivers."

Jonas: Rivers?

Father Michael: Yes. I haven't seen him since he left on his own. His mother was also an orphan here, the same time Barney still lived here.

Jonas: ...Amelia Rivers?

Father Michael: Yes. How'd you know?

Jonas: Because she's my mother...

A little while after Jonas had spoken with Father Michael and found out some big news for himself, he was taken to the cemetery that was down the hill before the lake, behind the church. In the center, surrounded by the graves, stands a tall concrete statue of an angel resembling in giving peace to the dead. This is where Amelia is buried. Jonas stood in front of her tombstone that reads "Amelia Rivers, June 16, 1946 – May 22, 1973." His grief and sadness aren't there as he was already numb.

Jonas: ...How did she die?

Father Michael: She committed suicide... The police found her in a tub of her own blood...

Jonas takes a slow breath and shakes his head with guilt and sadness.

Jonas: ...I should've at least been at her funeral.

Father Michael: It was a private funeral for her... I'm sure she didn't want you to see her in a casket...

Jonas: Yeah. Instead, I already see her in the ground...

Father Michael: I'm sorry for your loss, son... I promise you, she's now in a world of paradise with the lord.

Jonas didn't respond, but decides to move forward. Him and Father Michael walk just a little further past the graves, and reach Stoya Lake. The cold air from the calm lake blows softly in their direction and filled their ears with sounds of water lapping against the shore. They stand at the edge of the silvery water around grass shrubs, looking across the lake. Due from the heavy fog and steam, nothing is visible from afar.

Jonas: So this is where Barney liked to go?

Father Michael: Yes… The old water plant is just on the other side of this lake…

Jonas then notices an old rowing boat buried in the tall shrubs and covered with moss. It looks like it was left there for a while.

Jonas: Were the kids allowed on the water?

Michael: Only under supervision. On nice days, we'd take the boat out to go fishing. They loved it.

Other than the old memories and dull waters, there was nothing more for Jonas here.

A little bit later, as they're walking back up the hill to the church, Jonas sees a metal door on the backside of the building. The door looked lonely being under a small gable roof in the dark with a little bit of rust on the edges. It looks like it leads to the lower half of the church.

Jonas: What's behind this door?

Father Michael: That's where the children's rooms are... There was another entrance inside the church but it's been closed up... This door has been closed for a long time... After all the kids were gone, after Isaac... There's a key to it, but I don't know where it went... I never bothered trying to get inside. It would've been too painful... So it just ended up as an empty tomb...

Jonas stares at the door in thought to himself. He then remembers Father Michael mentioning a key. Jonas felt that the key he has brought him there to find more answers; more of the truth that lies behind this door.

Jonas: ...I think I may have the key...

Father Michael is confused by what Jonas said as he sees him pull out the key from his coat pocket. Jonas looks at the key just before placing it in the lock of the door. He turns the key hearing the heavy lock being opened. Jonas then opens the heavy door that leads into darkness, feeling the weight of it pulling him in.

Jonas: ...Are you coming?

Father Michael: ...No... There's nothing for me in there... Maybe you'll find what it is that you're looking for...

Father Michael stood still for a moment of thought, and he decides to leave Jonas alone. Jonas then looks back into the darkness and steps forward. Running out of clear view a few steps in, Jonas pulls out a small flashlight to make it easier to see. Ahead of him stretches a long hallway. The floor is a simple pattern tile matching with blue and white walls, and wooden doors on each side of the hall, symmetrical to each other. Each door is a room labeled with the names of the children that once lived here, some are open and some are closed. Jonas looks inside the rooms seeing something different in each one as he passes by, but everything seemed to have been left untouched for over a decade, ever since the children disappeared. The floors are still covered with scattered papers of child drawings, old coloring books, and some other debris lying around. Every room has the same appearance of dark walls and dark floors, all the small windows on the surface are stained with black dirt, most of the beds have fallen apart. The ceiling has some mold and mildew from endless leaks, leaving small dirty puddles on the floor. The further Jonas got down the hallway, the heavier the air started to get, and the more he felt trapped by the atmosphere around him. He could barely hear the draft from the outside coming into the long hallway, and then he started to hear the heavy door creak and shut behind him. The sound of the door shutting startled Jonas as he turns back to see if someone was there.

Jonas: Father Michael?

There wasn't a response, leaving Jonas to believe it was the draft that caused the door to shut. When he turned back around, he was startled again by an old music box toy he kicked by accident, hearing its rusted gears turn and break while playing a couple rough notes. With it being quiet again, he continued on strong, feeling a little more paranoid as he feels his surroundings trying to swallow him. Jonas then finally makes it to the other end of the hallway. There's a white door that separates it from all the others, which indicated it possibly being a room for a different purpose. The hard paint was peeling off of it and showing rust. He walks up to the door placing his hand on the doorknob and opens it up. It was an old boiler room. The room is pitch black with black dust and rust particles floating in the air glistening off of the flashlight. Looking further around the room, the walls are cement, covered with God knows what, there's an old chain link fence that stretches across the room that looks like a small dog pin for storage. The old boilers and pipes are all corroded. A small furnace door to one of the boilers was left cracked open, and there was something sticking out a little. Jonas opens up the door more to see what was inside. He then picks up a small torn cloth that looked like it used to be a part of a blanket before. Holding onto what was probably remains of a child's blanket bothered him a little, and he started to sense that some very bad things happened in this room. With not wanting to stick around longer, he leaves the boiler room. When Jonas made it back out into the hallway, he sees another closed door. On the door it had one label missing but one remaining, the label that's there read Isaac Rivers. Reading Isaac's name brought Jonas inside. There doesn't seem to be much of a difference in Isaac's room, it looks just as run-down as all the other rooms did. However, there is one thing out of the ordinary, and it's a fairly new red folder that is sitting in an old armchair. Knowing this was planted here for Jonas to find, he opens it up, finding notes that didn't make a lot of sense; it all was just a bunch of mumbo jumbo with lots of words and phrases scribbled out with ink. But then what stands out is a cut out picture of a woman from an old newspaper that was tucked away between the notes. Jonas immediately recognized the woman in the black and white picture. It's the face of the social worker, Harper Grayman. On the back of the small clipping is an address.

After seeing Harper's picture, Jonas knew he found another piece to the puzzle. He puts the picture back in the folder and notices some more writing on the back of the folder. The writing in bold ink reads "**ANOTHER IS GUILTY**." Jonas found what he needed and he takes the folder with him, getting the hell out of there.

A little bit after leaving the lower floor of the church, Jonas went to go find Father Michael. He's back inside the main part of the church calling for him, but there's no response. Jonas walks back outside to look, but there is no sight of the old priest anywhere. He didn't waste any more time. He found what he came there for, and he leaves the church. While Jonas is walking back to his car he tries calling Zach. The phone rings for a while, Jonas is getting impatient.

Jonas: Come on. Pick up!

A few moments later, Zach answers.

Zach: Hello?

Jonas: Zach. Where are you?

Zach: I'm just now leaving the Hagans. What is it?

Jonas: I found something while I was in the old orphanage. I have an address. 117 Crimson Clover Street. Meet me there, now.

Zach: Alright. I'll head that way.

Jonas hangs up and gets in his car in a hurry, fearing that Harper is in danger. He starts the ignition and shifts gears to leave the lot, glancing at the church just before driving away.

After leaving Alchemilla, Jonas is already on the road in a smaller part of town. He drives quickly and carefully, making it to the address on Crimson Clover Street. Parking the car in front of the house, Jonas gets out. Zach wasn't there yet, but Jonas knows it's too risky to wait. He quickly makes his way up on the porch of the main entrance. Jonas checks the layout, looking through the windows to see if anyone was home. There's no sight from what he can see from outside. He then knocks on the door asking for Harper.

Jonas: Hello?! Mrs. Grayman?! This is detective Jonas! I work with the police department!

Jonas knocks again, this time a little louder.

Jonas: Hello?!

No response is an automatic red flag for Jonas. He pulls his gun out from behind him, ready to enter. Jonas then opens the door and enters the home. The house feels empty by how quiet it is, but there's still another feeling running by. Jonas steps further inside, walking through the wide hallway and looking into the open rooms that connected all around him. Not a sound goes by, leaving him to believe either he got there just in time or he's too late. Walking further into another wide hallway, Jonas doesn't see any signs of an intrusion or signs of a struggle. While he's standing in the kitchen, he sees a light that's on in one of the rooms down another hall. Jonas makes his way to the doorway, entering with caution. He's in a bathroom with nothing to see inside, except a message that was written with blood on the giant mirror.

Blood Message:

THROUGH THE LOOKING GLASS

WILL YOU SEE THE TRUTH THAT DAY OR WILL YOU LOOK AWAY

WILL SEARCHING TAKE YOU HOME OR WILL YOU NEVERMIND THESE THINGS AT ALL

Jonas feels taunted by the suspect and these riddles. He then leaves the bathroom and checks the other rooms down the hall. Door to door, empty room after empty room, there's nobody inside the house. The blood on the mirror appeared fairly fresh, but there wasn't a body. Jonas is confused as he doesn't feel that he found everything here. He still keeps his guard up as he traces back through the house. Going back into the kitchen, Jonas sees a sunroom that's connected to the backside. He makes his way inside the large sunroom. Inside is an indoor pool where he finds his next dead victim, Harper Grayman. Her body is floating in dirty water of her own blood with her backside facing up. She was murdered, surrounded by her luxury and some baubles. Seen again, there are more lotus flowers that are floating around her corpse like she's in a water garden. Jonas wasn't happy to know that he was too late in this case. He then calls Zach, getting his voicemail again, and leaves him a message.

Jonas: Zach. I'm at the address. We have another dead victim. Adult Female. Possible stab wounds. And more Lotus flowers...

Give me a call. Let me know when you're almost here. I'll see if I can get a hold of Cyndy—

Jonas was shot twice in the back, catching him by a painful surprise. He stumbles a second in shock of the bullet knocking the wind out of him. Feeling a little weak, when Jonas turns around to see who was there, his vision becomes an interrupting blur. From what Jonas could see, they were completely dressed in black, hiding their identity. Time is slow for Jonas as he's trying to hold himself up. He then tries bringing his gun up, but the suspect is too close and stops him while piercing a knife into his abdomen. Jonas could feel the cold steel inside of him against his organs. He then felt the blade being pulled out in one quick motion, cutting him more again. Feeling exhausted and lost due to the amount of blood Jonas is losing, he fell back into the pool. Jonas is falling down again, just like before 6 years ago, the big splash from the impact of the water is cold. Deeper in the blue and red of the water and Harper's and his own blood, Jonas could see her lifeless face as he sinks down. The deeper Jonas got the more he started seeing black, his vision is fading in and out as he feels his body fighting to stay alive. Before getting too deep, he felt hands grabbing a hold of him and pulling him out of the water. Jonas could hardly move as he's being dragged across the wet tile all soaked. The suspect sits him up against the wall and pulls out a couple things they have on hand. What they have planned for Jonas is uncertain, but it's nothing good. Jonas is still blacking in and out, he could see the suspect preparing a high dosage of a drug from a vile with a syringe. When the suspect was ready for Jonas, he took his arm to give him the dose. Jonas grunts trying to resist, but he had no luck and no energy to do so. The needle is already in his skin giving him drugs already. Now cold and high, Jonas completely blacks out.

Later after Jonas was attacked, he's still unconscious. His eyes are closed; his clothes are soaked from blood and water. He could hear and feel more cold water from a showerhead running on top of him. Jonas remains still and helpless, lying quiet with himself.

A few moments later, Zach arrives at the address. He then quickly enters inside with his gun out and ready. Zach is on high alert as he checks his surroundings while looking for his partner, Jonas.

Zach: Jonas?!

There isn't a response. However, Jonas could hear Zach's voice, but he is too weak to move a muscle.

Zach: Jonas?! Where are you, Jonas?!

As Zach proceeds further into the house, he sees the victim in the pool. He could hear the showerhead in the bathroom, and he followed the sound.

Zach: Jonas?

When Zach opens the door, he finds Jonas unconscious while sitting in the bathtub in his own blood. Zach immediately jumped to Jonas's aid. While getting his clothes wet and blood on his hands in the process, Zach is using all his strength into pulling Jonas out of the tub. Jonas's deadweight brought him and Zach to the floor. Zach quickly took off his jacket and applied more pressure to Jonas's fresh wound. Jonas could no longer hear Zach's voice; just ringing. Everything has gone dark.

_____
_____

A lot of time has passed, everything is still dark. Jonas is staying in Aqua Heights Hospital. Everything started coming back to light in sense of Jonas's eyes. He could hear the heart monitor next to him which seems to be reading normal. After opening his eyes, he could see someone at the doorway talking to some others out in the hallway. Jonas couldn't tell who it is at the moment; his eyes are sensitive and his vision is still a blur. When Jonas moved to sit up, he felt a sharp pain causing him to be stiff. He pulls up the gown to see where his wounds are patched up and healing from surgery. Being distracted by his own self, he then hears the voice of a friend.

Cyndy: You're awake.

Jonas manages to sit himself up to see Cyndy in the room and sitting on the edge of the bed.

Cyndy: We were afraid you were never going to wake up.

Jonas: ...How long was I out?

Cyndy: 3 weeks... You lost a lot of blood. Zach kept you alive, long enough for the paramedics to get there... They said if he tried taking you to the hospital, you wouldn't have made it...

Jonas couldn't believe that he had been in the hospital for almost a month, and he hopes that it didn't hurt his chances in finding Eleanor alive.

Jonas: Where's Zach now?

Cyndy: He's talking to the town's council...

Jonas: The council? What do they want?

Cyndy: ...They want you arrested... Possibly serve a life sentence.

Jonas: What?!

Cyndy: Evidence was found. The knife that killed Harper has your fingerprints on the handle… The doctors here found cocaine in your system when they were doing blood tests.

Jonas: So they're charging me with murder?! The killer nearly killed me! This guy is clearly setting me up!

Cyndy: You haven't been charged yet. But I've been talking to them and they're having you remanded to Razorwail Penitentiary…

Jonas has no words but has his mouth and eyes left wide open from shock of the wrecking news.

Cyndy: Jonas?

Jonas finally speaks after his long thought in silence.

Jonas: …Do you think I murdered Harper?

Cyndy: No… Of course not, Jonas… I know you didn't do it…

Jonas sits there again in silence, anger, and fear of what will happen. Will he be able to get out of this mess or will he spend the rest of his days behind bars? Will Jonas be able to save himself before he can save his daughter? That's even if she's still alive. All these thoughts are intertwining inside trying to break him from what little hope he has left.

Cyndy: I promise I'm going to do everything that I can to get you out of this... Okay?

Cyndy then gives Jonas a heavy and warm hug, trying to make him feel not alone as he could barley feel himself hugging her back. In that moment, someone's knocking on the door as the door opens. Standing in the doorway is Kim. She looks like she was drained from worry as she walks into the room. Cyndy stands up feeling a little awkward, and she decides to give the two of them some space.

Cyndy: I'll- give you two some privacy...

Kim: Thank you...

Cyndy then left the room, leaving just the two of them alone. Jonas is even more surprised that Kim is here. Kim finally speaks and breaks the silence between them.

Kim: …How are you feeling?

Jonas: I uh- I've felt better… I'm surprised you're here.

Kim: Zach told me what happened, and I wanted to make sure you were okay. I've been checking in everyday…

Jonas: Oh. Well, I'm glad you're here… I am…

Kim felt a little warm by Jonas being glad to have her still around. It wasn't something she expected as she barely gave a shy smile. They both have a hard time looking each other in the eye and felt a little awkward from their presence as they're not used to the other being there anymore. Overall, they are both happy on the inside to feel a little bit of that connection they once had. Kim had then pulled up a chair beside the bed to be closer to Jonas.

Kim: It's like we've swapped places…

Jonas: What?

Kim: When we first had her?

Jonas: Hmph... 9 long months.

Kim: Felt like 13 for me.

Jonas: Yeah... But you were great. You both were.

The two sat there quietly in a moment of a breathtaking nostalgia, wondering where all those times have gone.

Kim: ...What happened to us, Jonas?

Jonas sat there slowly shaking his head not knowing what to say, even though he knew deep down inside.

Jonas: ...I screwed things up, Kim... If I drove us home like I should have that day, like I was supposed to, our little girl would still be here...

Kim's voice is tight and a little shaky as her and Jonas are finally opening up to each other after the long years.

Kim: ...I know you didn't mean for it to happen. You didn't know. How could you know? ...I blamed you for everything.

Jonas: You were right to, Kim—

Kim: No. No. I wasn't... I gave up from the start. I gave up on us when we needed each other most. And that wasn't fair.

Jonas didn't have a response to give, but before he could open his mouth to say anything, Cyndy walks back in. They both look at Cyndy as she didn't look too pleased.

Jonas: ...What is it?

Cyndy: ...They want me to take you, now.

Kim: They? Wh-who?

Jonas: The town's council... They're putting Harper's murder on me and having me remanded.

Kim: What?! They can't do that, can they?—

Jonas: Doctors found cocaine in my system, and they're trying to use that against me. To make it seem like I was high and out of control.

Kim: ...You can't go to prison...

Jonas: I don't really have a choice... Do I?

Cyndy: ...I'm sorry.

Cyndy is torn but is staying strong. Kim could barley hold herself together as she started to cry a little, feeling sorry and helpless for Jonas. Both Cyndy and Kim feel guilty not being able to do anything as Jonas sits still on the hospital bed feeling numb minded.

Jonas: Do I have clothes to change into at least?

Cyndy: Yes. They're in the restroom... Kim? Will you come with me?

Kim looks at Jonas sitting next to her. In her bloodshot eyes, all she could see is her husband, a simple man in his dying life. After so long of being lost in time, she felt inconsiderate of him, and all she could ask herself is "why?" She then leans over, giving Jonas a kiss on his cheek and hugs him tight as she's even more scared for his life. Jonas is lost again from Kim's touch. Cyndy puts her feelings aside, and Kim finally decides to go with her.

Cyndy: I'll fill you in on everything, later...

Kim: ...Okay.

Both of the ladies left Jonas to be alone. He sits there for a minute longer, and then gets up. When he stood barefooted on the cold floor his legs felt like noodles from being in that bed for so long. Jonas got his bearings and makes his way over to the restroom. He flips on the switch giving an ill-lit room, and he sees his clothes sitting on the bathroom sink.

After Jonas was already dressed and checked-out, everyone is outside the hospital. Cyndy is getting inside her car with Jonas already in on the passenger side. He looks and feels like this might be the last time he ever sits in the front seat of a car. Kim is in her vehicle waiting patiently and feeling nervous at the same time. When Cyndy drove off, Kim followed behind them back to the station.

Back at the station, after a couple hours, they're still waiting on further transportation.

Cyndy: I don't know why they wouldn't let me at least take you there myself!

Jonas: ...What can you do? Right?

The three of them sat there in silence until the sound of large squeaking wheels rolling in slowly brought them up.

Kim: ...Is that the bus?

Jonas: Yeah...

Nothing more was said and they all walk out of the office. Outside in front of the station is the prison bus. Jonas has already changed out of his regular clothes into his green prison clothes. The bus door is open to collect Jonas. Cyndy then starts putting cuffs on him.

Cyndy: Is that too tight?

Jonas: No.

Cyndy: Go on ahead. I will follow you up there.

Jonas just nods his head and moves forward and onto the bus where he's directed to his seat of placement. Kim and Cyndy are both heartbroken to see Jonas in the opposites on that bus in a prisoner's uniform.

Cyndy: I've already told Jonas that I'm going to do everything that I can to help him.

Kim: ...You make sure that he gets out of this. And you make sure to find the one responsible...

Cyndy agrees with Kim as she leaves to be out of the dreading sight. Jonas watches Kim through the thick window and feels the gears shift. The prison bus starts to leave and as it does, Cyndy follows it to Razorwail Prison.

Chapter 6: Stuck In The Inside

The prison bus that Jonas is currently on is driving miles and miles out from town. Up in the mountains is Razorwail Penitentiary. A large maximum security prison that is nothing but tall concrete slab walls. Jonas is looking out the metal sheeted windows as the bus rolls in on gravel ground, heading inside the prison. When the wheels stopped and screeched, the old squeaky doors of the bus open. All the prisoners look forward as a prison guard steps on. This prison guard looks like he's happy in his own way, to have newcomers.

Guard: Fresh meat! Welcome to Razorwail! A dead end for all of you miserable wastes of humanity! **LET'S GO! OFF THE BUS! SINGLE FILE!**

All the prisoners, including Jonas, all of them got up from their seats and got off the bus in order. Stepping out into the light rain, a few shotguns are aimed downed at them from a few guards up in the watchtowers. Jonas looks up at the rain clouds, feeling life becoming heavier like the thunder. He then looks ahead of him, in a line with the other prisoners. The head guard then gives further instructions.

Guard: Alright ladies! When we get inside, you'll all have your pictures taken for our system! So you better hope those smiles are white and perky, because you only get one! Now, let's go! Slowly!

Cyndy is parked off to the side of the facility. As she gets out of her car, through the tall barbed wire chain link fence, she can see Jonas at the back of the line walking with the other prisoners into the prison. She then makes her way inside the main entrance.

After entering the facility, Cyndy goes to speak to someone at the front desk.

Cyndy: Hi. I'm Cyndy. I'm the chief of the police force in Aqua Heights.

Woman: Can I see your badge? Please?

Cyndy pulls out her badge and hands it to the lady to verify it. The lady then hands it back.

Woman: Okay. What're you here for Cyndy?

Cyndy: I'm here to see someone.

Woman: Who is it you're here to see?

Cyndy: Jonas Rivers... He just arrived here today.

Woman: All of the new inmates aren't able to have visits or anyone to see them on the first day. You'll have to come back in a few days.

Cyndy: A few days?

The woman didn't respond, but just left the conversation at that. Cyndy is not pleased, but rather disappointed and frustrated. She knows there's nothing more she can do today, so she leaves with a little bit of worry, but she'll be back in a few days.

Meanwhile, at the prison entrance for new inmates, Jonas is having his picture taken. In his green prison jumpsuit, as a number and not a person, he stands at his height with defeat. Looking bad for himself, he feels everything caving in as he can hear steel gates clicking and opening up.

Guard: Face the left!

Jonas then faces the left for them to get the view of his side. First mug shot in his life, now on record. Once that was done, he's then ready to join back with the other convicts.

A little later on, back in line like kindergarteners, they're all walking down a long stretched hallway with some separate holding cells along each side. While walking down, the newcomers are taunted by the veteran inmates.

00959525: Don't be shy fellas! I'll make you comfortable in here!

00979725: Bring one of those sorry bitches my way! Hey!

00020225: It's not the same in here as it is out there! Nobody in here cares about you!

Everyone wants a piece of the fresh faces, liking all the attention they can get. Jonas ignores them, only hoping that none of them recognize him.

After being goaded the whole first day, Jonas is finally taken to his cell.

Guard: 01070725! This is your cell!

Jonas then steps inside his cell. The barred gate closes behind him.

Guard: Don't get too comfy, Jonas. Feds don't last long in here. Especially ones like you... Better hope you can sleep tonight. You're gonna need it.

Jonas feels even more uneasy knowing that this particular guard seems to already know so much about him. He knows that he's even more vulnerable now. When he looks out his cell window, he didn't see much but a giant wall behind it and some tree lines of a mountain over the top. It continues to thunder, and Jonas then sits down on the side of his bed thinking to himself, just wondering how things are going to play out.

_____
_____

Sometime on the second day, the same guard approaches and enters Jonas's cell.

Guard: Alright, you! Get up!

Jonas is just barely awake, and was confused why he's being taken out of his cell.

Jonas: What's going on?

Guard: Don't ask any questions! And just do what you're told!

Jonas didn't argue with him as he didn't want any more trouble than he is already in. He gets up on his feet, walks out of his cell, and does as he's told.

Guard: This way.

Jonas moves ahead with the guard watching him from behind.

After leaving his cell block, they're walking down another hall with little to no surveillance. Jonas feels a little bit of tension. Other inmates that were mopping the floors watch them as they're walking by, knowing something. The guard loses a little bit of his patience.

Guard: Eyes front! Keep walking!

A few more steps down, they take a turn down another hallway. No one is in sight, and Jonas started getting more anxious.

Jonas: Where are you taking me?

Guard: …Here…

The guard then opens up a door for him. Inside is the woodshop. The room isn't being used.

Jonas: What am I doing here?

Guard: You have some friends waiting.

Some other inmates come out from hiding in the back of the room. There are five of them, and Jonas recognized one.

Kess: Jonas! I'm glad we could finally meet again! Thank you, Scott, for bringing him to us!

Scott: Keep my name out of your goddamn mouth! Or I'll send you all to the infirmary! I'll be waiting outside! You guys have 5 minutes!

Kess: 5 minutes will have to do.

Scott, the guard then closes the door behind Jonas. And he knew that what's coming next isn't going to be fun.

Kess: This is a big switch of things, for you I'd say. I'm happy to see you, Jonas.

Jonas: I'm afraid I can't say the same, Kessinger. Except that I'm glad you're still in prison.

Kess: Well, I won't be much longer. I've been promised to be let out of here early for "good behavior."

Jonas: Pfft. Who promised you that?

Kess: Somebody that wants you hurt.

Kess then throws a punch into Jonas's stomach, knocking out every breath in him. Two of the other inmates then hold Jonas back up, restraining his arms, keeping him from defending himself. Kess throws another hard punch across his face, and another, and another. Jonas is getting dizzy from all the hits to his head, and his entire mouth is bleeding with blood coating his teeth. Kess punches him again in the stomach and takes a step back, letting the two inmates behind him get a few hits in. Getting hit from each side, beat raw, fists coming in back to back, Jonas is dropped down to the floor. His body is hitting the hard concrete letting up saw dust and dirt. Not even a chance to hold himself up, Kess throws a kick in his side, bruising him up some more. Kess then grabs him by the hair to say a few words.

Kess: Lucky for you. This ain't a death sentence... I've been told specifically not to kill you. But who knows. Maybe I will.

After Kess stood tall again, he got another kick in before their five minutes was up. Scott had then opened the door back up for them to clear out.

Kess: That was a good first session... I'll see you again, real soon, Jonas.

After Kess and the others left, Scott approaches Jonas on the floor.

Scott: Get up. On your feet. I'm taking you to the infirmary.

It was hard for Jonas, but he slowly gains enough strength to get back up for Scott to escort him back out. One other prisoner is waiting patiently for Scott's instructions.

Scott: Clean this up.

The inmate then starts cleaning up whatever little bit of blood may have spattered on the floor, getting rid of any trace of what happened as Scott takes Jonas to the infirmary.

Later, after being beat up, the doctor is just finishing up with Jonas.

Doc: A few bruises and some minor head trauma. But you'll have an easy recovery.

Jonas: Easy? Right...

Doc: You'll stay here the rest of the day. Incase anything shows up. But other than that, you'll return back to your cell, first thing tomorrow.

Jonas is sitting up on the bed in the infirmary room with others in worse shape. He didn't care. All he wonders is if things are going to get worse from here on out. He started talking in his head.

Jonas: "Will I be able to find Eleanor? Am I ever going to find her? I'm trying... I need to get out of here first. I have to hold on as long as I can... I just hope for something good. And soon..."

_____
_____

A couple days later, in the morning, Jonas is interrupted from his sleep by Scott.

Scott: Did I wake you, Rivers? Rise and shine cupcake. You actually got a visitor for you today.

Jonas gets enough energy to bring himself up and out of bed and on his feet. His appearance has started looking more lazy and uncared for. He's still feeling sore from the second day, on top of being tired from lack of sleep. His cell door then slides open for him.

Jonas: You sure this isn't another one of "my beatings?"

Scott: Not today. There's a woman here to see you... Seems that you still have people that care about you...

Jonas steps out of his cell and the gate closes behind him. He waited for further directions.

Scott: Just give it time. And eventually, you won't… However long your time is?

Jonas didn't say a word. He just wants to go see someone that isn't part of the prison. Him and Scott then walk together through the concrete walls and metal bars of hell.

A little bit later, Jonas is finally let into a small separate room by another guard. When he steps inside, he sees Cyndy standing across the room. Both of them are happy to see each other, and Cyndy quickly steps in to hug him. As soon as they hugged, the guard monitoring from outside detained them from contacting.

Guard: No touching guys!

Cyndy and Jonas know the rules, but it didn't stop Cyndy from being annoyed by the guard's ignorance.

Cyndy: I'm sorry. I wasn't able to see you when you first got here. They wouldn't let me.

Jonas: It's fine... Where's Zach? I figured he'd be here too.

Cyndy: He went back to Harper's home to try and find more evidence that'll prove you didn't commit the murder...

Cyndy is just now starting to notice some of the bruises on Jonas's face.

Cyndy: What happened to you Jonas?!

Jonas: I took a beating my second day here... I've got people after me in here too... I don't think the word has fully gotten out yet, that I'm a FED. But it won't be long until that happens.

Cyndy: Can you get protective custody?!

Jonas: I don't know. A guard named Scott, has his eyes on me right now. He's the one that helped arranged this beating to happen... He had to have been tipped off with some information about me, so whoever killed Harper could keep tabs on me... Kessinger is somehow involved too. I don't know... I doubt I'd be able to get protective custody that easily... Even if I did, would I be safer?

Cyndy: Stop. Don't talk like that. I promise I'm going to get you out of here Jonas. Just hold on.

Jonas: ...Yeah. It's easy for you to say. You're not the one that's stuck in here...

Cyndy feels heartbroken with nothing to say in return.

Jonas: ...If you want to get me out of this alive. Don't say anything that I told you to anyone. It's going to take time. And that's what I need to survive in here...

Cyndy started feeling more sadness and guilt for Jonas's safety, but she knows that he's right. The guard outside then opens the door to end their visit.

Guard: Time's up! Let's go!

Jonas looks at Cyndy one last time as she watches him leave the room with the guard.

A little bit later, Jonas makes it back to his cell, and he just watches the gate close again for the rest of today.

Sometime the next day, Cyndy is back in Aqua Heights. She's currently talking to one of the town's councilman in regards of Jonas.

Cyndy: There's no full explanation that links up with Jonas being Harper's murderer!

Councilman: Chief. There have been multiple cases, which you and your members have not been able to close. More murders and missing children have been happening recently, and it's causing the town problems. Everyone is scared, and questions why the police force haven't been doing their jobs in protecting their children.

Cyndy: I understand, and we're doing everything that we can right now! But Jonas is not just a civilian here! He's an agent that has served the town for over a decade. We've worked together almost 13 years now! And he's not just a colleague of mine, he's my best friend, and I'd trust him with my life!

Councilman: In Jonas's case, not only was he just a suspect, but he's had some personal history with Harper, which you didn't bring up in your report. Did you lie because you were trying to protect him?

Cyndy: What? No, I didn't lie. What're you talking about?

Cyndy has no idea what's being brought up, and is completely unaware of this information being given.

Councilman: These are reports from year 1968.

The councilman hands Cyndy the papers from thirty years ago to look through. She hasn't seen or heard anything about this before.

Councilman: Mrs. Harper was a social worker who separated Jonas from his birth mother, 30 years ago.

Cyndy: I read his files before, and I've never seen these.

Councilman: It could be that he had his own personal agenda at the time. Therefore, he lied and kept some personal documents hidden.

Cyndy: No. This isn't something Jonas would do.

Councilman: The bottom line is that Agent Jonas cannot be trusted. But I'm curious, chief. Are you to be trusted? ...You have a lot of weight on your shoulders right now. I'd be more careful and wise with your decisions. This conversation is done for today.

Cyndy feels like she's being personally attacked by the whole town all of a sudden. She didn't speak about anything else, and she leaves the councilman alone, for now.

A few moments later, Cyndy made it outside the town hall. She then gives Zach a call. The phone rings, and she manages to reach him.

Zach: Hello?

Cyndy: Hey. I just talked with a member of the town's council.

Zach: Did you have any better luck?

Cyndy: Not really.

Zach: Hmph. That figures.

Cyndy: What about you?

Zach: I'm back at Harper's, right now. I've searched through everything... There's nothing here. I'm going back to the old watermill. See if there's anything we missed there.

Cyndy: Okay. I'm going back to the station. I've got some things I need to look over.

Meanwhile, back at Razorwail Prison, Jonas is lying in bed in his cell, waiting for the rest of the day to pass. It isn't long until Scott came back to his cell to pull him out.

Scott: You got another visitor.

Several minutes later, Jonas walks back into another small room, expecting to see Zach or Cyndy. Instead, it's his friend Walter, the old man that he met back at the tavern. Jonas is just as surprised to see him as Walter is to see him in prison-wear and handcuffs. They then join each other at the table in the middle.

Jonas: Fancy seeing you here.

Walter: Yeah. Well, I read the papers, seeing it mentioning you going down in a dark part of history of this town.

Jonas: You can't believe everything you see, Walter. Those papers are usually just cooked up for good storytelling. It's just the same old glitter story.

Walter: Why are you here?! Jonas?! What got you into this mess?!

Jonas: ...Why do you care, Walter?

Walter became just as annoyed as Jonas.

Walter: Don't do that. Jonas... Just tell me what's going on... Why did you need my dog that day you came by on your own? ...You better tell me something, dammit. Or I won't be going back home.

Jonas didn't speak for a moment. He sits there thinking, he can just end the visit and go back to his cell or tell him the truth. Jonas trusts Walter, but is hesitant by his own self.

Jonas: ...I uh... I'm looking for my daughter, Walter... I've been looking for her for 6 years...

Walter didn't say anything. He just listens.

Jonas: She was only 7 when someone took her from me... I did everything I could to find her... And when the trail went cold, my wife left me... But I kept looking and looking. And still, nothing... And then 6 years later, I got new leads that told me she's still alive...

Jonas started getting teary eyed from all the haunting memories flowing back. But he keeps sharing more with Walter.

Jonas: That day I came by your house... I wanted to take Bogie because I believe I was close... and I thought he'd be able to help me find her...

Walter is taking it all in, and feels nothing more than a little bit of guilt. Jonas continues letting out more for him.

Jonas: ...All that's happening now is all connected to me for some reason... And right now, it's trapped me here... I didn't murder that woman, if you were wondering... And I'm not sure what I'm going to do, or what I can do... I'm just someone that wants to find their kid... Whoever is making this happen... I have to play by their rules to do that...

Walter still didn't speak. There was nothing to say. Jonas then stands up and starts walking to the door for the guard to let him go back to his cell. Once the guard opened the door, Walter quickly speaks.

Walter: Jonas!... I hope you get out of here... And I hope you find your daughter...

Jonas: ...Thanks... I hope so too...

Jonas proceeds down the hall with the guard, leaving Walter to be able to go home with his freedom. It starts to thunder outside as a storm is making its presence.

Later, back at the station, Cyndy is looking through the old reports that the councilman gave her about Jonas's past connections with Harper. She's learning a few things about Jonas that no one else knew. Some of it is irrelevant, but a lot of it was personal, such as family relatives, and foster homes. It wasn't long until Zach walked in her office, drenched a little from the rain. He seemed to have something.

Cyndy: Anything from the watermill house?

Zach: Actually yeah... Under some of the floorboards, I came across this...

The evidence that Zach has is in a plastic bag. He places it on Cyndy's desk in front of her to see for herself. She looks at him with surprise as she's able to investigate further with the evidence that they have.

Meanwhile, at Walter's warming home, he's sitting in his office. His life is staring at the computer screen again, not knowing what to write. Bogie is resting beside him, afraid of the storm. Walter pets Bogie to comfort him, and to comfort himself from another storm. An ugly storm that's pulling his friend in it.

Later, at the prison, the storm is right over it. Dark storming night clouds, crashing thunder, flashes of lightning, downpour rain. Scott is walking down the main block, hearing the thunder above him. His uniform shoes are stepping in puddles on the hard floor from the heavy rain that's leaking through parts of the ceiling. Scott makes his way up the stairs and onto the 2nd level. He walks down the catwalk to the last cell on the end, which is Jonas's cell. Jonas is sitting on his bed, reading some book and waiting as if he already had a feeling that Scott would be coming to pull him out of his cell again. And he was right.

A little bit later, Jonas is brought to the showers. The room is loud and feels like a sauna. A lot of the showerheads are running hot water, creating enough steam to fog up the security cameras. Jonas knew he was being set up again. Scott takes out his baton and tosses it on the floor for him to use as he leaves the room, shutting the doors behind him. It's already hard enough to see from all the steam. The small security lights and the lightning from outside are the only source of light he has. He then hears another set of doors open up from the other side of the room. Jonas is tensed up as Kess and two of his inmate friends are back to beat him some more. Seeing them again, Jonas quickly grabs the baton off the floor, being as ready as he could for what's about to go down. Kess and the others then rush towards him. Being ready to fight back, Jonas swings at the first two that is closest to him and manages to hit them down. With Kess rushing up, Jonas acts quick by lunging his foot at Kess's chest, kicking him back with part of the wind knocked out of him. Having the blood pumping, the adrenaline, fight for survival. Jonas is filled with it all as he charges back at Kess to beat him down. Before Jonas could get a second hit on him, one of the others grabs him by the looseness of his jumpsuit. Acting like animals, Jonas throws an elbow in the other inmate's face in another attempt to get to Kess, but he's then quickly grabbed again by both of the other inmates. They're having a hard time holding onto him, so they throw him down to the wet floor, kicking him on both of his sides and stomping on top of him. Jonas had let go of his only weapon of defense as he's trying to shield himself on the ground, taking the hard hits mainly on his ribs and back. Once Kess got back up, he sees the baton that Jonas had dropped. He picks it up off the ground to use on Jonas.

Kess: Get him up!

They pull Jonas up off the floor and slam him back into the tile wall. Lightning strikes and lights up the room as the thunder roars loudly. Kess pulls out a small towel and wraps it around his hand and wrist to keep a hold of the baton. Jonas still struggles in the hands of the inmates.

Kess: Hold him still!

With anger and no holding back, Kess takes a swing at Jonas's mid-section, knocking the wind out of him. He hits him again, making him cry in pain. Scott continues to stand just outside, counting down the minutes as he can hear the tussle and the beating behind the closed doors with no one else around to stop it.

In that same time, Kess hits Jonas back in the stomach, causing him to cough up blood from the hard blow. Kess then went for his legs, and he yells in more pain as he falls to his knees. Bleeding heavily from his mouth, as Jonas looks up at Kess, he took the final hit across his face, making him hit the floor hard.

After Kess was done beating Jonas almost to death, he tosses the baton back on the floor. They leave him out cold on the wet shower floors, soaked from blood, sweat, and water. When they walked out of the showers, Kess looked at Scott for him to take care of the rest. Just like that, another night on the inside is over.

Next day, the morning is almost over. Cyndy is a little tired from her work as she didn't leave her office last night. Looking through some of Jonas's lost files; she hasn't had the chance to look over the things that Zach brought to her yesterday. Instead of now, she puts the bag of evidence in her purse for her to look through later. She's leaving to go see Jonas at Razorwail.

About an hour later, Kim is at Razorwail hoping to see Jonas. She sees an officer at the desk to make a visit.

Kim: Hello. I'm here to see Jonas Rivers?

Officer: What's your name?

Kim: Kim Rivers...

Officer: Are you his sister?

Kim: I'm his wife—or um.. ex-wife. Sorry.

The officer doesn't acknowledge Kim much as they're pulling Jonas up through the computer.

Officer: He's not going to be able to see anyone right now.

Kim: Why not?!

Officer: He's currently in the infirmary.

Kim: Infirmary?! What happened?! Is he okay?!

Officer: I'm sorry. I can't give you any information on that. You can try again tomorrow or give us a call.

The officer wasn't being much help to Kim. She couldn't think. She didn't know what else to do except what little they told her. Kim got a little anxious for Jonas's safety. Deep down, she still cares about him. She starts to feel a little lightheaded when she decides to leaves.

Moments later, Cyndy is walking inside through the doors and runs into Kim on her way in. They're both caught off guard to see each other.

Cyndy: Hey, Kim? What're you doing here?

Kim: I was just trying to see Jonas.

Cyndy: Why couldn't you?

Kim: They said he's in the infirmary. I asked them what happened, but they wouldn't tell me.

Cyndy couldn't believe what Kim was telling her. Without saying a word to Kim, she goes to speak to the officer herself.

Cyndy: Excuse me? I need to see Jonas Rivers.

Officer: You can't. He's in the infirmary. Someone else had already asked.

Cyndy had already lost a little of her patience with the officer. She pulls out her badge and holds it up to the window, outranking them under intimidation.

Cyndy: I'm the Chief of police at our headquarters in Aqua Heights! I want to see him now!

The officer didn't ignore her or her badge. They unlock the door ahead for her. Before she went further, Kim catches up to her.

Kim: They're letting you in?

Cyndy: Yeah. I'm gonna see how he is…

Cyndy didn't say more to Kim as she goes to see Jonas. Kim doesn't know how she feels; sad or frustrated. There was nothing more that Kim could do, so she just watches the doors close and lock behind Cyndy.

A little later, Cyndy is deeper inside Razorwail Prison. Some more secured doors are unlocked for her to proceed further. It's a labyrinth of halls that can easily make you feel lost. She finally makes it to the infirmary and enters. Cyndy sees a few inmates in bed, but she doesn't see Jonas yet. She walks a little further down to see Jonas behind a curtain in his own bed. He has a few bandages, some stitches on his face. Recovering in his sleep, Jonas looks to be out of it from the medications and life conditions inside Razorwail. Cyndy's very upset with herself not feeling like she's working fast enough to get him out of this. She asks a medical staff that's nearby, about Jonas.

Cyndy: Excuse me? Can you tell me how he is?

The staff member checks the log attached to Jonas's bed and reads her some details.

Nurse: He had a broken rib, some heavy bruises, and bad cuts on his face... This inmate was putting up a fight. These injuries would've probably been a lot worse or fatal, if he didn't. I guarantee it.

The nurse goes to check on other patients, leaving Cyndy alone with Jonas. From his injuries and life in prison, she's terrified. Nothing but bad things keep happening, and it puts a lot of weight on her shoulders. All of things, from her losing her first child to now, between trying to get him out of Razorwail alive and finding his daughter. It's all putting her in a depressive state, because everything seems to be falling apart and is just getting worse by the minute. Cyndy clears up a bit and walks over beside Jonas. She looks at him with such endearment, and she places her hand in his with great tenderness. Jonas is still asleep with the warmth of a close friend nearby. Cyndy's in thought about his past and asks in a low voice.

Cyndy: ...Why didn't you tell me about you and Harper? ...And your mother?...

Jonas didn't respond, and Cyndy couldn't wait. Other than knowing that he's still breathing, there's nothing else she can do for him right now except let him rest. She leaves the infirmary, and then leaves the prison. Getting back in her car, she looks in her purse to see the bag of evidence still there. Cyndy had no answers for the questions she wanted to ask. She's leaving Razorwail to go back to the station to continue further work alone.

Meanwhile, Kim is just now getting back home, pulling into the wet driveway. Home sweet home with no one to come home to. She's walking up to her door and lets herself in. Kim sits down alone in the dining room. She starts to rest her face in her crossed arms on the table. With a short glimpse of something, she peeks over across the table. A tiny black box is sitting across from her on the other side. Kim is confused by it being there when she's never noticed it before. She walks over and picks it up to get a closer look. Kim opens it to find a ring inside. It wasn't hers, and she started getting uncomfortable by the feeling that she's being watched. She checks all the rooms and closets, even the attic, and no one is found inside the house. Taking no chances, she checks all the windows, locks all the doors, and goes to the master bedroom. Kim locks herself in, hoping she makes it through today and night.

Concurrently, Zach is at home, and he's been drinking again. An open capsule and some prescribed pills are lying on the nightstand. He's in his room, on edge over his friends and his job. Everything is getting the best of him. He doesn't know what to do and he's feeling unhinged. Sweating bullets, talking to himself, he hears voices. Zach is talking to the voices.

Zach: Please. No! I don't want to! Please don't! You're hurting them!! No! Don't hurt me!

Something falls and breaks in his kitchen. Zach quickly turns to the noise and is on high alert. He quickly grabs his gun that he had lying on the bed and has it aimed. Zach has a tight grip on his gun as he walks down the hall to the kitchen. Being ready for someone, there's no one in the kitchen. The small drapes on his kitchen window are being blown by the outside wind. A glass vase had fallen and shattered on the floor due from the strong wind that was blowing on and off through the open window. Zach goes and closes the window that he left open. There's no sign of an intruder in his home. He's constantly feeling paranoid from all the horrible things that's been going on in Aqua Heights. And it's taking a big toll on him and his friends.

Later, it's getting dark out. Cyndy pulls up at her second home at the station. She walks in, no one is there. Everyone else is home with their families as she's back at work. Cyndy walks into her office. She closes the blinds for privacy and she puts her purse down on her desk. Cyndy gets a text from Kim.

Text From Kim:

Kim: Can you come by tomorrow morning?

Cyndy replies that she'll be there first thing. She then sits on the sofa to catch her breath from today.

At the end of the night, Jonas is still in the infirmary and is still recovering while he sleeps. Everyone waits their time away in their own affairs.

Chapter 7: Out of Tether

It's now morning of the next day. At the station, Cyndy had stayed the night in her office. She wakes up from her sleep and slowly gets herself ready. When she was proper enough, she grabs her gun and purse and leaves to go to Kim's place.

A little bit later, Cyndy is pulling in the driveway at Kim's and parks behind her car. She steps out and walks up to the door. Cyndy knocks, and it wasn't long after that Kim opens the door. Kim is relieved to see Cyndy.

Kim: Hey.

Cyndy: Hey? Is everything okay?

Kim: I- I don't know…

Cyndy: What is it?

Kim has Cyndy follow her into the house. While she's looking around the place, Kim brings her the ring that she found yesterday. A cold chill runs through Kim as she explains.

Kim: When I got home yesterday, I saw this sitting on the table... It's not mine... I don't know how it got there. I couldn't sleep... I spent all night just thinking about it... Someone had to have been here...

Cyndy also thought it was strange. She looks at the ring and sees a name engraved on the inside. The name on it is Amelia Rivers.

Cyndy: "Amelia Rivers."

Kim: Who?

Cyndy: It's the name on the ring... She's Jonas's mother... Do you not know her?

Kim: No... I've never met her. Jonas never talked about his parents... He never talked much about his past...

Cyndy was surprised that Jonas never mentioned his mother to Kim before.

Kim: Is she alive?

Cyndy: No... She died years ago...

Kim: Oh... Does he have any more relatives? Anyone left in his family alive...

Cyndy: He has a brother... But no one knows where he is...

Kim didn't have anything to say. She feels like she doesn't know anything about Jonas. There's nothing but silence between them. They both are trying hard to figure out the puzzle pieces, but nothing is solved to why this ring was brought here. Cyndy then hears her phone buzz. She pulls it out to see that she has a missed call from Zach. Cyndy tries calling back, but she's doesn't reach him. She tries again and the call is a busy signal.

Cyndy: Dammit... I gotta go. I'm gonna take this with me. Are you going to be alright here?

Kim: Yeah... Yeah. I'll be fine.

Cyndy: Okay... Stay safe...

Kim: You too...

Cyndy takes the ring with her and leaves. Kim watches her from the front window of her living room as she's getting into her car. Starting up the car, Cyndy can see the worry and loneliness on Kim's fragile face. She shifts the gears in reverse, backs the car out of the driveway, and leaves Kim's home to go find Zach.

Sometime after leaving Kim's, Cyndy arrives at Zach's place. She pulls in front of his house and gets out of the car. Zach's car is still in the driveway, so he couldn't have left for work or anything else. Cyndy looks around to see if anyone is watching her, but she didn't see anybody. She then walks up onto the front porch and knocks on his door. No one answers. Cyndy knocks again, hollering for Zach.

Cyndy: Zach! It's Cyndy! Let me in!

She waits patiently, but she decides to let herself in once she noticed that his door was unlocked. Cyndy is walking in slowly, and she doesn't see Zach around. Something feels off to her as she calls for Zach in the living room.

Cyndy: Zach?!...

With all the danger that's been happening recently, she takes no chances and pulls out her gun. Cyndy has her gun close, her finger off the trigger, but ready to take action. She remains calm in her profession as she enters the hallway, having complete focus. A few steps down, she can hear a showerhead running, just like Zach did at Harper's place. She calls for Zach again.

Cyndy: Zach?!

After a few moments of silence, she hears Zach's frail voice coming from the bathroom. He calls for Cyndy.

Zach: ...Cyndy...

Cyndy hurries to the closed door of the bathroom. When she opens the door, she finds Zach in the tub with a fresh stab wound and cold water running over top of him. He was left and found in the same manner as Jonas. She quickly turns off the running water and goes to aid Zach. He barely speaks.

Zach: I'm okay. Just call an ambulance...

Zach rests his eyes and Cyndy doesn't waste time. She pulls out her phone to call for help.

Cyndy: This is Chief Cyndy! I need an ambulance here at 1438 Marigold Street!

Following from making the emergency call, she pulls a towel off the towel rack to apply pressure on Zach's wound. Looking around while waiting for help to arrive, she sees another message that's left on the bathroom mirror written in more blood. Cyndy reads the message.

Blood Message 2:

IS THIS THE LIFE TO TAKE

TO BE FORCED TO BREAK

ALL THE PAIN YOU CREATE

Another time around the same day, Jonas makes it back to his cell. Some inmates that were waiting in his cell jump him. Catching him off guard, he takes some hits. Jonas is being thrown hard into the cement walls and is then held down on the floor while being gagged with a sheet to keep him quiet. He couldn't break free as one of the inmates pulls out a shank.

00050525: The word is out in here about you being a FED... Killing you is gonna build my reputation-

Jonas got enough strength to headbutt the talking inmate, shutting him up.

00050525: You stupid piece of shit!

The inmate is pissed with his shank clenched in his fist as he quickly comes back to end Jonas. When he had the shank up to his neck, the sound of guards and their whistles are saviors.

00050525: It's the fucking PIGS! Come on!

The inmates are highly aware and they move quickly out of Jonas's cell before the guards showed up. Jonas catches his breath as he sits himself up and realizes that was a close call. He's in more danger, now that the word is out. Jonas doesn't know what he's going to do, but he knows that he has to figure something out fast.

A couple hours later, at the hospital, Cyndy is in a waiting area. A doctor then comes out to see her. She's stressed with high attentions of concern.

Cyndy: How is he?

Doctor: He'll live. His wound wasn't as bad or deep, and was a lot easier to repair than your other friend before.

Cyndy has some relief from the good news, though it seems that her mind is mostly somewhere else.

Doctor: He's in his room resting. But he's fully capable to talk, so you're more than welcome to see him.

Cyndy is barely paying attention as she's thinking of other things, but she acknowledges with a response.

Cyndy: No. Sorry... No. That's okay. I'll come back later.

Cyndy then leaves the hospital, and when she got in her car she knew she had been putting off what she needed to do. She looks at the evidence bag again. Inside it is a room key to room 321 at Bloom-Weather Apartments. The car is put in drive and she leaves the parking lot.

Meanwhile, at Angel Side Diner, Kim is back at work on her shift. She's walking around on the floor, picking up dirty plates from the bar and booths, collecting her tips along the way. Her thoughts are troubling her as she walks to the back, placing the dishes in the kitchen sink.

Kim: I'm taking a smoke break, Joyce!

Kim steps out the back behind the diner for a smoke. She lights herself a cigarette to calm her nerves and mind, feeling like she's headwire. Walking down the side and out to the front of the diner, the main road is ahead of her. Kim can just feel that her life isn't the way it used to be. How empty inside she's become, how things aren't the way she dreamed for them to be. Kim remembers days when it took so much more to get her down. She takes up every inch of the cigarette as she can, all the way to the end, taking inches off her life as she did the past six years. Coming down the road, in a breath and cool breeze, she sees Cyndy speeding by. Once she was gone, Kim breathes out the last bit of smoke before heading back inside.

In the meantime, at Razorwail Penitentiary, it's lunch hour. Jonas is in his cell and has been grinding a toothbrush of his on the edge of his bed for the past hour. All the cell doors begin to open to let the inmates out. Jonas finishes up with making a shank, and he stores it in his pocket for now.

Shortly after, Jonas is in the cafeteria with all the other inmates. He's constantly looking over his shoulder, keeping his eyes open. Waiting in line for food, Jonas sees Kess and a few of his friends staring him down as they chow down on their meals. They aren't the only ones; several others have their eyes on Jonas too. He can feel the pressure from all the eyes locked on him. Jonas collects his food from the counter and he walks off to sit down. Everyone keeps looking at Jonas, talking about him and how he's a uniform outside the walls. He manages to find him a seat, and he sits down alone, keeping to himself. Jonas takes small glances around the room as he eats his lunch.

A few minutes in, as Jonas is eating, the same inmate that tried to kill him in his cell ends up sitting down in front of him with a little evil smirk on his face. Jonas is staring him down ready for anything he might try to pull. He slowly places his hand in his pocket where he has the shank. The troublemaker then opens his mouth to speak.

00050525: You think you can blend in and be like us in here? You're not like us. And you can't call for backup in here either… Enjoy that last meal of yours… It's gonna be coming out of you after I slice you open.

Tension is rising. Jonas and the inmate look like they're about to have a showdown. Suddenly Jonas gets up quick to make a move. The other inmate is up out of his seat too, and stops Jonas from using his shank on him. All the other prisoners are watching. With the inmate being up close and having a hold on his arms, Jonas has him right where he wants him. Acting quick, Jonas turns the shank on himself, stabbing his right leg multiple times. The targeted inmate's eyes open wide as he watches the shank drop on the floor with Jonas falling down, screaming in pain as the prison guards are quickly making their way.

00050525: I didn't do that!! I didn't do that!!

All the prisoners in the cafeteria are riled up from the fight and all the excitement. The prison guards break them up, taking the inmate away as he yells at the top of his lungs, knowing he was set-up. Jonas is then being taken to be cared for.

A few stitches later, after Jonas had his leg cared for, he's placed in protective custody. Away from general population, this cell block has less lighting and is a lot quieter. Directed by the prison guards, Jonas is brought to his new cell. When they opened the door, he limps inside. Closing the thick heavy door behind him, Jonas didn't show much expression by it. He feels a little bit of relief to be in his new dark cell. Jonas lays down his thin foam mattress and blanket on his new bed, and he lays down himself to get more rest. He didn't fall asleep, but just stares up at the ceiling and the light from outside his small window. Jonas remembers days when it took so much more to slow him down.

Back on the outside, Cyndy is at Bloom-Weather. She steps inside and passes by the counter by the entrance. No one is there at the moment, but she notices all the extra room keys in the back. All the extra keys are hanging in there racks, except for 321. The rack for that room is empty, but she has a key.

Some floors later, Cyndy is walking down the hall as if she was going to see Jonas in his apartment. Across from his room 320 is room 321. She pulls out the key not knowing what she's going to fine or if she's going to find anything. Before opening the door, Jonas's neighbor, Iris sees her.

Iris: I've never seen anyone go into that room before... You're Jonas's friend... You two worked together. Right?

Cyndy: Yes... Who are you?

Iris: My name is Iris... I'm his neighbor. I'm right next door... I haven't seen Jonas in a while. Is he okay?

Cyndy: I hope so...

Iris: Is he going to be coming back?

Cyndy: I don't know... That's why I'm here... I hope to bring him back...

Iris: Me too... Jonas was always good to me and my son... He was always good to us.

Cyndy: Yeah. Jonas is one of the good guys. He's a good man...

Iris: Well, it was nice talking to you…

Iris says no more as she goes into her apartment, room 318. Cyndy then looks back at room 321, and then inserts the key. She turns the lock and opens the door. The apartment was still a little furnished. Most of the furniture in the living room was covered with sheets. The air is thick with dust, the wallpaper is withered. No one's lived in this apartment for thirty years. Cyndy looks around in the kitchen. When she turns the faucet on the rusted sink, no water comes out. There's nothing of use or interest from the cabinets. The fridge doesn't work, but she finds something resting inside. It's a VHS tape. Cyndy takes the tape out of the fridge. She looks to see an old TV in the living room, and she has the idea to use it. Pressing the power button, it took a few seconds, but it turns on and still works.

After the TV is turned on, Cyndy is hesitant of what she might see, but she pulls herself together and places the tape in the VHS player. The TV screen flashes bits of light and colour. The video playing has a grainy picture to it. It's compilations of different sights of different places. It shows previous victims, before they died and after. First was April, then there was Eirene, and then in a short moment an old photo of a little boy popped up and was gone in a second. The video is then showing places they've been, from the river by Blue Creek Park to Aberdeen Watermill, then Alchemilla Orphanage and the lake. Bloom-Weather is then shown, the footage shows in bits of the person filming making their way inside the building and up the stairs onto the top floor. They're walking down the hallway, stopping in front of room 321, the video freezes. Cyndy gets a little paranoid and looks at the front door as if what's on the screen is about to come inside.

The video connects back again, skipping to them being inside the apartment. Cyndy eases and continues watching. In the video they're just looking around, and then it cuts to the bathroom showing nothing but an empty tub and a blank mirror. It's very bright due to the lighting and poor quality. The video then stops, cutting into a static. Cyndy thought it was over, and she's about to eject the tape until another part came up. She sees what else the tape has to offer, and it does of course have something. The tape is then showing Harper's home, and them entering inside. From the cameras perspective, the person recording is hiding in another room as they watch Harper looking out her front door to see if anyone was there. Harper closes the door being completely oblivious of it and she walks to the sunroom where her body was later found. The one recording follows her. Once they got close, as soon as Harper turns around, life drained from her face as she starts to scream. The video skips over the gruesome murder, showing her body floating in the pool.

After seeing Harper dead, Cyndy then hears someone else entering the home and the camera shakes in a hurry, and it cuts off again. When the video played back up, she can hear Jonas making the call for Harper's murder. Cyndy is watching from the killer's eye, watching them slowly come up on Jonas. She covers her mouth trying to hold her breath as she sees them pointing a gun at his back. When she sees the gunfire she tenses up, and she quickly turns it off. Cyndy is a little shaky and she had a couple of tears stream out of her eyes. She wipes away the tears, then takes out the tape and places it in her purse.

After the horror that Cyndy watched, she looks around the apartment more to see if there was anything else she could find.

There's nothing in the bedroom, all that's left is the bathroom. She turns on the light inside and immediately recognizes it. The empty tub and the blank mirror are the same from the video. There's a rusted color stain that's circles around the inside of the tub, a high level ring from liquid that sat around for a while. If Cyndy had to guess, it would be blood, but she doesn't know fully what it represents. Like everything, she knows it's connected. Jonas and Zach were both found bleeding in tubs, and there were messages left on the mirrors, but the mirror in this apartment is blank. Cyndy then takes a closer look at the mirror. She begins touching the mirror, feeling around the edges, and she notices the looseness. The mirror is able to come off, and in a hole in the wall is something that was hiding behind it. It's an old letter from Barney and an old photo underneath. Cyndy sits on the edge of the tub to read the letter.

Barney's Letter:

"A few years back,

I was there again.

Watching the calm waters.

Stoya Lake.

I remembered us being younger together.

Not a care in the world,

but only for each other.

Now, it's been just me…

Sitting alone in 'our spot'…

Without you here…

Without you here

to be with me.

But you left.

And now, you hold the love

for our two sons, away, leaving me out.

I know I've hurt you.

And you nor they will ever forgive me.

I wish that I could change.

But I can't save you two from it.

I feel so numb and dumb

sitting there, now here…

Even now, it's not the same.

I still miss you so dearly.

But I'm scared, Amelia.

I'm terrified that you'll never

be missing me.

Whenever you last saw me.

I could tell how uncomfortable you were…

I don't know if you

got tired of me…

Or maybe I just frighten you…

But I'm sorry.

Just know that

even after today.

I'll always love you.

Even though it's a shame we've had

to disappear. I wouldn't have it

any other way.

I know you're gone.

And you'll probably never

read this, now that you're not here.

But I'll say goodbye.

One last time.

I hope you don't forget me.

But I also hope you don't

remember this moment.

Remember our good times together.

All the other moments we've shared.

I hope you found some happiness with me.

I'm sorry...

But now that you're free,

I won't feel numb anymore.

Amelia...

You were my true love and miracle."

After reading the letter, Cyndy looks at the photo. It's a faded picture of Stoya Lake on a sunny day. Some lily flowers are seen with a row-boat resting on the bank of the lake. She takes a moment, and glances at the note and photo before folding them up and putting them away in the pocket of her jacket. She found what all there was to find, and she may just have what she needs. Cyndy then gets back on her feet, and she exits the apartment. Looking back into room 321, she closes the door. Cyndy starts to lock it back, but decides to leave it. When she's about to head out, she then sees Jonas's apartment right across from her. Cyndy remembers the two of them and their little moments together. She then proceeds to walk down the hallway to leave, and goes to pay another visit with the councilman.

Later, after Bloom-Weather, Cyndy is back at the town hall. She's speaking to the same member of the council from before. Cutting to the chase, Cyndy hands them the tape and apartment key.

Cyndy: Going back through our previous sights. We found the room key hidden away at the old Aberdeen Watermill House, a few miles northeast, a little bit away from town. When we found the key of course, it belonged to one of the rooms at Bloom-Weather Apartments… That key goes to the same room Amelia and Jonas lived in 30 years ago… That's where I found this tape… And I think you need to see the tape for yourself…

The councilman took Cyndy very seriously, even more serious than before.

A little bit later, Cyndy is walking out of the town hall. Shortly after, she gets a call from Kim again. She answers the call.

Cyndy: Kim?

Kim: Hey, Cyndy…

Kim is just now getting off work. On her end, she sounds worried. Cyndy can tell.

Cyndy: What is it? Kim? Talk to me…

Kim: I just got off the phone with someone at the penitentiary... Jonas is in protective custody...

After preparing for the worst news, she quickly catches her breath. Cyndy is then feeling relieved and even smiles to herself with a small chuckle.

Kim: What?

Cyndy: He's away from the other prisoners... No one can touch him there... He did it...

Kim didn't fully understand, but Cyndy is happy with the timing and ease.

Meanwhile, Jonas is still in protective custody. He's standing up against the cold walls of his cell, waiting and waiting for the time to pass. Jonas then walks up to his small window to look outside. He stands there looking out at the tree-sides hilling down the mountains. The skies are still grey, the season of fall remains, steaming fogs cloud further down in the trenches of the forests. Nothing is sound where Jonas is. He then slowly walks over to his bed and sits down. Jonas is alone without the sunrise. Sitting quiet in his cell, he has no choice but to waste the day.

Later on during the day, Cyndy is back at the hospital visiting Zach. She's sitting across the room, watching him mumble in his sleep. He eventually wakes up from shock. Zach notices Cyndy in the room as he's clearing his head.

Cyndy: Hey…

Zach: Hey…

Cyndy: Bad dreams?…

Zach: Yeah…

Cyndy: Do you remember what happened?

Zach: Other than the pain. No. Everything was just white… How are things going with Jonas? Is he okay?

Cyndy: So far… He's in protective custody right now.

Zach: Oh, that's good.

Cyndy: Yeah. I'm waiting on a call from the councilman. I saw them earlier today... I'm hoping for something good.

Zach: ...Well, I'm sure it's all gonna work out...

Cyndy: Let's hope so. I don't know what else we can do at this point.

Zach: We'll keep fighting... Has the doctor said anything about my release yet?

Cyndy: He said that he still wants to keep you in for at least another two weeks.

Zach: Oh, goodie.

Cyndy: I think it's a good idea.

Zach: Cyndy. I can move. I'm fine.

Cyndy: It's not up for discussion. You stay here. That's an order.

Zach: *sighs* Alright. Fine.

Cyndy: …I'm gonna go. I'll come back in a couple days.

Zach: What am I supposed to do?

Cyndy: Rest. I'll see you in a couple days.

Cyndy then leaves the room for Zach to rest and fully recover. Once she was out of the hospital, as she's walking to her car, she hears her phone buzz. She quickly answers it.

Cyndy: Hello?… Yes… Oh my god! Thank you… Thank you so much! This is the best news I've heard in a while… Hey. I need a favor… I need some paper documents from Razorwail… The names are "Scott Yeckery" and "Kessinger Reeves…" A few weeks?… Okay, great. Thank you…

Cyndy hangs up the phone. She has anxious thoughts as she recovers herself, taking deep breaths. Some good signs might arrive. One breath at a time.

Later at night, at Razorwail, Jonas is still in his holding cell. He's just lying there on his bed, casually carving words in the wall.

Jonas finishes up, using the only source of lighting he had coming from outside into the inside. He stops writing on the wall, and just stares up at the cracks in the ceiling. A couple moments of silence, a note is slid under his cell door. Jonas noticed it, and then he hears Scott's voice as he sat up in his bed. He didn't move a muscle. He just listens and keeps quiet.

Scott: Is it lonely in there? Jonas? Do you miss us?... 'Cause we sure do miss you...

After nettling Jonas once more, Scott carries on down the block. Jonas feels that it's safe now. He gets up from his bed and retrieves the note that Scott left. He then walks over to the window to read it. The note has no name of who it's from. It's a short message.

Prison Note:

YOU THINK YOUR SAFE IN THAT NEW CELL

WE'RE STILL GONNA GET TO YOU

THERE'S NO ESCAPING IT

The message is quite simple and clear. Not like everything that goes on behind these walls. Jonas doesn't react much, but crumbles up the piece of paper and tosses it on the ground. Out of tethering webs, and he can already feel himself being pulled back in. He goes back to the window and looks outside, and wonders how much time he has left. "How long until he's back in general population?" "How long before he's ambushed again?" "Will he die in prison?" Jonas doesn't know, except that his days are numbered. There is no escape. It is just a matter of time.

Chapter 8: Amounted Mountain

YEAR 1980

In the year 1980, at Alchemilla Orphanage. On one bright and sunny day, smiling children are being brought back to shore from the row-boat. One by one jumping out of the boat and running up the hill. Their guardian, Father Michael shouts as he's climbing out of the boat last.

Father Michael: CHILDREN! H-HOLD ON!

All eleven children are running ahead of Father Michael, laughing with each other with more excitement as they run past a young man standing by. The young man has a little smile of joy as he watches the children run by. One of the children spoke quick as they just about knocked him over.

Child: Hi, Barney!! Come on, Isaac!!

In a flash, the children were long gone continuing up the hill towards home. The oldest kid of the bunch is walking past Barney. He didn't say anything, but Barney acknowledges him.

Barney: Hello, Isaac.

Isaac looks at Barney, and he didn't respond. He just gave a weak smile and continued walking. Father Michael is then approaching Barney.

Father Michael: Isaac's not much of a talker. Neither were you… But give him time and he'll be an open book with you.

Barney: Well… I just came down here to tell you that all the light fixtures have been replaced. I also cleaned out the gutters. I think I'm gonna go now.

Father Michael: You should stay for dinner! And today is movie night! I got the projector set upstairs! Come on! It'll be fun!

Barney: Yeah? Well… I guess.

Father Michael: Excellent! I'm happy to hear it!

Father Michael pats Barney as he walks past him. Barney stays for moment longer. He looks out at Stoya Lake feeling comfort from his memories. After a moment to himself, he turns around to the trees and walks back up the hill.

Another night in the year of 1980, it's storming out at Alchemilla Orphanage. The storm isn't letting up. Lightning constantly lighting the night and forests, thunder is beating heavy soundwaves into the mountains, and the downpour from the clouds above is drenching the soil. Down at Stoya Lake, someone is getting off the row-boat and is pulling it up on shore. They begin stepping in the mud making their way up to the orphanage.

Concurrently, at the orphanage, Isaac is waking up the other children. He puts his finger up to his lips and tells them to be very quiet. All the kids leave their beds and their rooms and follow Isaac down the hall. They go into the boiler room and pile in behind the storage fence. Everyone stays close and listens to the storm roaring outside. One of them is listening for something else.

Meanwhile, somebody is at the door outside from the opposite end of the hallway. They turn the knob and open the door. Walking down the hall looking inside all the empty rooms, they continued forward. They're getting closer and closer to reaching the boiler room.

At this time, the children can hear footsteps from down the hall until they stopped right outside the door. They all keep quiet; hoping whoever it was would leave. The door then suddenly creaks ajar. Looking into the darkness, the children are quivering with fear as the door continues to open. Whoever it was, they step inside. Everything is ominous to the children. The visitor then closes the door of the boiler room to keep everything and everyone quiet.

Hours later on the same night, back at Stoya Lake, Isaac is by the shore. He's standing there cold and drenched in the rain with his feet in the mud. The visitor is bringing the row-boat back onto the bank. They then walk over to Isaac as the thunder roars in their steps. Isaac is shaking in fear as they stand in front of him. The heavy rain and storm made everything harder to see, but when the lightning strikes, the boy can clearly see Barney's face. His eyes look tired and angry. Barney looks at Isaac and then grabs him by the collar of his shirt. He drags him vigorously through the mud and sand and into the lake. Barney then starts submerging the boy under water. He's standing over top of him, being aggressive with the child. Barney occasionally brings Isaac up to catch a quick breath, then immediately pushes him back under. Every second of air is instead lungs choking on dirty water. Isaac holds onto every partial breath that he could as he's plunged under the black water over and over. Life and death, cleansing away sin, like a brutal baptism, full immersion. The sound of the stormy night fades in loud then fades out quiet, air and water, over and over, again.

TODAY

A few weeks later, at Razorwail Penitentiary, Jonas is resting in his cell. It's early morning, the blue hour of the day, and he's awakened by a loud thud on his door. He could then hear Scott's voice.

Scott: Hello, Jonas! Today's the day! You get to come back and join us! Aren't you happy?

Jonas didn't respond. He knew his time was up.

Cyndy: Capt. Scott Yeckery!

Cyndy is on the same cell block with a few other officers and prisoner Kessinger Reeves. They're all making their way to Scott and begin making his arrest.

Scott: What is this?!

Cyndy: Mr. Yeckery. You're under arrest for the abuse on the inmates, corruption, and misconduct. I have documents here with false signatures that were out of your jurisdiction and they were also not approved by the warden or any medical staff. Your abuse of power and organizing criminal activity is over. You and Mr. Reeves here are both being transferred out of state today.

Kess: What?! I had nothing to do with any of this! This is all his doing!-

Scott didn't say anything, but he stares down Cyndy with a lot of anger inside of him. There's nothing left of him to defend as he lets everything turn over, and he's put in handcuffs. They're then both escorted out, and Cyndy continues her business.

Cyndy: Open 412A! Release!

Shortly, the door is unlocked, and it slowly opens up. Jonas is standing inside waiting to see a friendly face. He slowly steps out of his cell and in front of Cyndy. She gives a soft smile as she asks.

Cyndy: You ready to leave this place?

Jonas's eyes lit up a little in signs of hope and redemption. He looks at Cyndy, and he nods and says—

Jonas: Yes.

Jonas walks down the cell block as an inmate one last time, leaving with Cyndy. Another hell left behind, along inside Jonas's cell, he left a message on the wall that said "IT'S QUIET HERE."

Afterwards, Cyndy and Jonas are back at the station. Jonas is in the men's locker room putting real clothes back on again. It feels good but also strange to be back on the outside, after Razorwail. He takes a moment to breathe then closes his locker. When Jonas came back out of the locker room, Cyndy is there waiting for him. She has two things to return to him, his badge and his gun. Jonas takes back his belongings, small parts of his life. The two of them stand in front of each other again, reunited.

Cyndy: It's so good to have you back. Jonas…

Cyndy then leans into Jonas, hugging him gently and holding him close. Jonas then puts his arms around Cyndy. They hold onto each other for a good while. Once they let go, things cleared up more between them. Jonas is happy to be out of prison, but he still has something he needs to do. He's still looking for his daughter.

Jonas: Where's Zach? Did you find anything more on finding Eleanor?

Cyndy: We did find a few things... Zach's in the hospital-

Jonas: What?!

Cyndy: He was attacked in his home. I found him, the same way he found you at Harper's...

Jonas: Is he okay?!

Cyndy: He's fine. They should be letting him leave soon... But we need to be more careful about this, Jonas... All of us...

Jonas didn't speak, but he understands. Cyndy isn't wrong.

Cyndy: Come on. I'll show you what all we've found.

They go into Cyndy's office. She digs out a couple things from the drawers and sits them on top of her desk. One of the things was the ring that belonged to Amelia, Jonas's mother. Jonas picks up the ring.

Cyndy: Kim found that in her home one day...

Jonas: Kim?... Is she okay?

Cyndy: Yeah. She reached out to me and I saw her the next day... She was scared and confused, but she wasn't harmed... That's was on the same day when I found Zach at his place...

Jonas looks back at the ring. He knows it's all connected to him. But how? What does his mother's ring represent? Why did Kim find it? Does it resemble Kim and Jonas's marriage? Something dear that's gone? All the questions are whirling inside Jonas's mind. Cyndy then hands him Barney's letter.

Cyndy: I found this in Amelia's apartment... That man at the old watermill, he knew her... Zach found her key in the floorboards...

Jonas sits down in the chair in front of her desk, and he reads the letter. A lot of history unfolds for him as he reads further, uncovering more of his past, seeing blinded connections of his mother. The more he read the more pain he endured. He then folds up the letter, staring off in space. A lot of anger and sadness is building up inside of Jonas. This letter seems to be the only closure he has for the death of his mother.

Jonas: ...She was murdered... My mother... It wasn't a suicide, like they said...

Jonas sat there quietly after learning more about Amelia and Barney. Cyndy didn't know what to say but—

Cyndy: I'm sorry, Jonas…

He didn't speak; he didn't even look at Cyndy. Jonas is wrapped up in his mind. He can feel some of the feelings being unwind. All this time, huge parts of his life was in grey area, left behind to find. Cyndy then brings him the photo that she found with the letter. He holds it to see.

Cyndy: This was with the letter…

Jonas immediately recognized the picture. The boat, the lake, the flowers; he knows the location.

Jonas: This is at the orphanage! The water plant is just on the other side of this lake! That's where this picture was taken!

Jonas rushes up from the chair to leave.

Cyndy: Where are you going?!

Jonas: There. To the water plant-

Cyndy: I'm not letting you go alone!

Jonas: You should go see if Zach is okay.

Cyndy: No! You're not going alone! That's an order!

Jonas stops and looks at Cyndy. He has every intention of going against her order.

Jonas: Then meet me there! Make sure Zach is okay, and he'll come too! I know it! I know it's been crazy and we've had a lot of close calls! But I don't have a lot of time left! It might already be too late! But I've gotta see this through!... I need to find Eleanor!... I need to find my kid!... So if you wanna take away my badge, fine!... She's there... I know it. I can feel it... You can arrest me when this is over...

Jonas removes his badge and lays it on Cyndy's desk.

Cyndy: Jonas?!...

Jonas walks out of her office not looking back. Cyndy froze. She wants to go after him, but she knew she couldn't stop him. His mind is made up.

After walking out of the station, Jonas got in his car. He quickly starts it up and leaves the lot to go to the old water plant. Cyndy is standing there in her office holding Jonas's badge. She didn't know what do. Jonas is driving through the town, and no one is in sight. The streets and sidewalks are completely empty, it's the strangest thing. The steam has become heavier and is fogging up everywhere. Things are changing, but for better or worse?

Shortly after Jonas had left, Cyndy does the same. She's going to the hospital, and hopes to catch up with Jonas afterwards.

At this time, Kim is at home taking a shower. She's standing still feeling the hot water getting lukewarm. Remembering her and Jonas holding each other, she remembers feeling that closeness. Kim misses it. She misses love.

Then, Jonas is driving past Blue Creek Park. He looks through the passenger side seeing where he and Eleanor use to spend time together. Where he'd push her high on the swings and spin her on the merry-go-round. He hears their laughs, thinks of their smiles. Jonas can feel his insides tearing apart as he'll always remember that day, where the tragedy started.

Same time, at Walter's, he's sitting in front of his piano with Bogie lying beside him. A small glass of hard liquor is resting on the wooded cover of the instrument. He's playing soft notes with melancholy in the air around him. The dog whimpers. Walter's attention is then drawn to him. He lets him outside to do his business. While Walter waits on the front porch, he grabs the newspaper off the floor. He ganders through the pages and reads where it mentions Jonas's release from Razorwail. Walter has a form of relief in his eyes as he sees that his friend's innocence was proven, but he still has worry in his heart.

Now, Jonas is miles out of Aqua Heights. He's driving back on the long lonely road that's covered in rainbows of graffiti. In the countryside, at the top of Baleen River, down the hill through the fall-winter trees he can see the old watermill. Nothing from that place but anger, more pain, and disappointment fueled him.

Concomitantly, back at Bloom-Weather, Iris is walking down the hall with her son to her apartment. She stops at her door, and looks at room 321. Iris then looks at Jonas's door, and she thinks of him. She then looks at her son and gently rubs the top of his head, keeping him close again as she opens the door for them returning home.

Finally, on the road to the orphanage, the road splits. Jonas takes the back road on the right, and it takes him further through the woods. It's getting harder and harder for him to see because of the steaming fog. The road began to feel more rough and unbalanced. He didn't want to crash, so he stops the car. His radio is muffling static again, so he knows he's close to Alchemilla Orphanage, which means the water plant isn't far. Jonas gets out of his car and walks from here on. Walking a few ways down the road, he could barely see ten feet in front of him. A little further, Jonas knocks off some gravel into a big drop below. He caught himself just in time, saving him from a nasty fall. Parts of the road was completely washed out, it's just a mist of steam he can see. The gap is too big to clear a jump, but a small side of the road and hillside is still intact and is wide enough to cross. Jonas is able to make his way around. As he's getting closer, he sees a large sign off to the side that reads "Hybrid Fountains Water Plant." After seeing the sign, Jonas started sprinting forward. He's panting as he reaches a gate in front of the plant. The gate is open, and Jonas makes his way through. The water plant is just ahead of him. He looks around before heading inside. Jonas can see the lake and lilies on the grassy wet slopes. From the victims, the flowers, the photo, this place. It's all connected here. Jonas makes it to a door that's unlocked. He pulls out his gun as he opens the old heavy door. It leads into the main office of the facility. Jonas is looking around, but it's a little dark in some places. Day from the outside shines through the old office rooms which lit up the hallway. Rubble and dust covered the floors. The building is slowly falling apart. Down the hall, Jonas notices that one of the rooms looked different. He walks inside, and there are lots of associations of a child, more particularly his daughter. The room is themed from Eleanor's heart and imagination. There's an old bed, lots of drawings on the walls that resemble her memories, a picture of her old home, drawings of her and mom and dad, a green colored rocket shooting up to the glow in the dark stars that cover the ceiling.

Jonas: ...This is where she slept?

Jonas then hears something from down the hall. It sounded like music. He leaves the room to go and investigate.

Meanwhile, Cyndy arrives at the hospital. She's up on the third floor and walking through the halls. Cyndy makes it to Zach's room, but when she looks inside, he wasn't there. She looks around thinking he might be in the restroom, but no one is in there either. Cyndy is confused and worried about what's going on, and then she sees Zach's badge on the nightstand next to the bed. She picks it up wondering where his whereabouts are. Is he in trouble? Was he released early? Did someone find him? Cyndy didn't know, but she can't just stick around, so she leaves to find Jonas.

Back at Hybrid Fountains, Jonas is exiting the offices and entering into the plant. Catwalks up high and rusted machinery tower over them in this large room. The roof is a big sky window that made everything easy to see. The music echoes louder in the distance as Jonas is getting closer. He can make out the sound clearer to his ears. The room then opens up a lot more, big enough to have a ballroom dance. Ahead is a wooden table with a plate of food and a cup of water. Jonas then sees at the end of the room, a girl playing on an old worn out piano with a long chain that's shackled on her ankle and a pipe on the wall. The tune she's playing is familiar to Jonas. It's the same tune Kim played back when he first met her. Jonas feels heavy as he stops to hold himself up. He then calls out to the girl.

Jonas: ... Eleanor?...

The girl stops playing, and she quickly turns around to see Jonas. She stands up quickly, not knowing what's going on or why or how Jonas is here.

Jonas: Eleanor? ... Honey? ... It's me...

The girl stands still. She didn't know how to react. Her face looks like Eleanor's, but she's not a little girl anymore. After six years, she'd be thirteen now, and about the same size as this girl. Jonas walks to her slowly. He puts the gun aside and kneels down in front of the girl looking into her eyes. Jonas tears up as he sees his daughter up close. He then hugs her and holds her close. She's still standing still, but she then hugs him back, and she finally speaks. There's a hint of sadness in her voice.

Eleanor: Dad?

Jonas immediately looked up at the girl with excitement sparkling in his eyes after hearing her voice.

Jonas: Yes! Baby! It's me!

Eleanor begins to cry in relief of her long agony. Jonas quickly hugs her again, giving her that affection she had long missed.

Jonas: Oh baby! I'm sorry! I'm so sorry! I'm here! I'm here now! Come on! Let's go home!

Jonas grabs his gun and shoots the chain to break Eleanor free. He puts the gun away and is ready to take Eleanor away from this place, and get her home. As he's about to turn around and leave with his daughter, he can feel the barrel of a gun at the back of his head. Jonas didn't make any sudden movements. He is surprised when he hears his friend's voice.

Zach: I'm glad you're finally here, Jonas.

Zach takes Jonas's gun that he had tucked away. Jonas turns around to look at Zach with a lot of questions in his face. He doesn't understand what's happening.

Jonas: Zach?

Zach: Not quite. Brother.

The word "Brother" is digging into Jonas.

Jonas: ...Isaac?

Isaac: Rivers? ...Yeah. Full blood... A family reunion... You know? Putting myself in the hospital for you wasn't easy, but it was necessary... Please sit...

Jonas sits down at the table facing towards Isaac.

Isaac: Eleanor? Honey? Go sit next to your dad.

Eleanor listens to Uncle Isaac, and she sits down beside Jonas.

Isaac: I'm sure you have a lot of questions.

Jonas: You have no idea.

Isaac: Oh, I'm sure I do. Jonas... But I'm also pretty sure a lot of those questions were already answered for you. You just haven't put all the pieces together...

Jonas: So why all this?... Why you?

Isaac: I've been asking myself that question all my life. "Why me?"

Jonas: Those people you murdered—

Isaac: "Those people" tore apart our family—

Jonas: What about those kids?! Andrew, April, and Eirene?!

Isaac: I didn't want to hurt them! What about the kids at Alchemilla?! **Laura, Carol, Piper, Anna, Bella, Alex, Ethan, Curtis, Wyatt, Graham!** No one seemed to care about them! ... It's because of him!... He made me watch... Then he'd make me hurt them... I was punished every time I didn't listen... My friends! My other brothers and sisters!... They're all gone. They weren't spared. They weren't given a chance... You were lucky.

Jonas: What're you talking about?

Isaac: Harper... She had me taken away when I was born... My mother didn't even get to hold me in her arms... I'm sure she made our mother believe she was going to get you back... Of course, that was a lie... Before the orphanage, I was put in a home. I lived there 'til I was 8 or 9... The woman that lived there, beat me. She was an addict. She'd make me take whatever she was taking. One day she forced a needle in me. I was high when child services found me. I was aggressive and scared. They placed me in another care facility for young kids that are supposedly violent or crazy... That's where Father Michael found me. You remember him? But unfortunately I wasn't lucky enough to even have a good home there at Alchemilla... The night my friends were killed, dad brought me to mom's apartment... He told me why he let me live. He told me a lot of things. A lot of things I wish I didn't know... Growing up, I never knew who I was or who he was, you or our mother... I knew nothing about the life that I wish I could've had... I guess it was fate. Huh?

Isaac takes Jonas's revolver and looks at the cylinder chamber. He then opens it up to see four cartridges left. Isaac then takes out three bullets and leaves one. He spins the chamber, hearing the clicks as it comes to a complete stop. A man sport of roulette is about to take place.

Isaac: You lived in 1 or 2 homes?

Jonas: ...2...

Isaac: I bet they were nice homes. Were they?

Jonas: They were... Good people too. Both homes...

Isaac: So where are they now?

Jonas: I don't know... I haven't seen them in years.

Isaac: Did they forget about you? Like you forgot about your past?

Jonas: I didn't forget. I just put it behind me.

Isaac: Is that what you did with mom? You just moved on.

Jonas: I didn't carry that burden all my life.

Isaac: That's because you just got to live on! Jonas! I lived her burden everyday! I didn't get a break! Never! But it never broke me... You were lucky enough to come out of everything I've put you through. All the curves and corners you had to cut. I'm impressed that you made it out of Razorwail. You were even able to find your daughter, alive... Six long years, everyone else gave up, but you didn't... You went through hell to find her, and you did... Luck is on your side Jonas... It never really was on mine.

Isaac then aims the revolver at Jonas.

Jonas: Isaac! Listen to me! There's no need to do this! Just walk away from this and let Eleanor and I go!

He pulls the trigger and nothing happened, but it scared Jonas and Eleanor.

Isaac: My luck has already ran out. Jonas… Eventually, yours will too.

Isaac opens the chamber back up and places another bullet in it. He does the same thing before, and he spins the cylinder again, with two rounds this time. As he aims the gun back at his brother, Jonas's phone rings.

Isaac: Who's calling you?

Jonas pulls out his phone and sees that Cyndy is calling.

Jonas: It's Cyndy.

Isaac: Funny how she always calls you, but not me... Go ahead. Answer it.

Isaac keeps the gun on Jonas as he answers the phone to talk to Cyndy.

Jonas: Hello?

Cyndy: Hey?!

Jonas: I'm at the water plant... I found Eleanor... She's alive...

Isaac pulls the trigger. Jonas flinched real hard, but again, the gun didn't fire a shot.

Cyndy: Are you alright?

Jonas: Listen. Call for backup. Get here as quick as you can. Please.

Isaac pulls the trigger again and Jonas flinches for the second time. It was another click without fire. Jonas can then see the tip of a bullet through the cylinder loading in the chamber.

Cyndy: Jonas?! What's wrong?! Jonas?!

Jonas: I'm sorry.

In a split second, Jonas rushes forward at Isaac as the next shot was fired. Eleanor screamed from the loud gunfire. All Cyndy heard on the phone was a gun shot. She couldn't hear anything after that.

Cyndy: Jonas?! Jonas?!! Shit!

Cyndy floors it as she's already on her way to the water plant. She still has a few miles.

Meanwhile, the gunshot had missed Jonas. He manages to tackle Isaac down, disarming him of the revolver from the fall. Jonas tries holding him down as Isaac grabs and claws at his face. Eleanor backs away in fear.

Jonas: Eleanor!! Run!! Go!!

Eleanor hesitates, and she didn't know what to do. She doesn't want to leave her dad. Isaac then punches Jonas off of him to break free. He pulls out his 9mm Beretta to use on Jonas, but Jonas is quick enough to get to him, and he kicks it out of his hand. The gun slides away across the ground a few feet. Jonas climbs back on top of Isaac to keep him down. He throws a punch and another across his face. Isaac is bleeding out his mouth, and he gained the strength to push Jonas off of him again, but Jonas kept on his feet to come back. Isaac kicks him back hard and he fell up against the table then hit the ground hard. Eleanor stays back afraid. Jonas tries picking himself back using the table next to him. Isaac crawled over to his gun, and when Jonas stood up, he fired a couple shots and hit his chest and midsection.

Eleanor: No!! Dad!!

Eleanor screamed as she watched her dad get shot. Jonas fell back down against the table, catching himself with what little strength he had left in him. Isaac walks over towards him. He's watching his older brother bleeding out and reaching for a small knife that's lying next to a plate on the table. Isaac then grabs the knife off the table and fiercely stabs Jonas's hand, pinning it to the table. His daughter screamed more out of fright as he screamed in pain once he felt the blade pierce his flesh and bone. Jonas is struggling. He tries using his other hand to pull the knife out.

Isaac: It's sad seeing you like this. Jonas... But you and I, our lives have a sad history... It'll be over soon...

Jonas screams again as he finally pulls the knife out of his hand. He then turns to Isaac, staring up at him with sympathy.

Jonas: ...I'm sorry. Isaac...

His little brother tears up a little as he points his gun back at him. Before he could pull the trigger, he was shot in the back of the head. Blood splattered across the table and Isaac fell down. Jonas's body is going into shock. He can see Eleanor standing in front of him shaking from trauma as she's holding his gun. Isaac is lying dead on the floor. Smoke is coming out of the barrel of the revolver. She finally lowers the gun, whimpering and trying to catch her breath. Jonas could hardly move, he couldn't speak, and could barely see. While help is on the way, his daughter drops the gun and crawls up beside him. As they're sitting up against the table together, side by side, she holds onto him as he holds onto her, waiting for help to arrive.

_____

_____

A week has passed after the water plant. Jonas is under care at the hospital. He's in a coma. His daughter, Kim, and Cyndy are all there. Eleanor is sitting by the bed looking at her dad as she held his hand. She's never seen him like this; she's always seen him strong. The machines monitoring Jonas's heart rate are slightly normal, and it's the only sound filling the room.

Cyndy: I'm gonna get some coffee. Do you want anything Kim?

Kim: Sure... Ellie? Would you like something to eat?

Eleanor: No thanks...

Kim: I'll get her something for later. In case she gets hungry.

Kim leaves the room with Cyndy for a little bit. Eleanor is left alone with her dad. It's just the two of them like before. She sniffles quietly and speaks.

Eleanor: I'm sorry. Dad... I'm sorry this happened to you... I was so scared. It was so lonely... I was strong though... But it was so hard... I'm sorry for what I did. What I did to Isaac... He never hurt me... He was nice to me. But he wouldn't let me go home... I feel sick... After what happened... I didn't think I was ever going to see you or mom again... I wish you were awake. I hope you can still hear me...

Eleanor could feel his hand barley clench hers. She knows he can sense her there, but his eyes never open, and he doesn't speak back. His heart rate is slightly decreasing. The beats are slowing.

Eleanor: Dad? I just want you to know that I love you...

She looks at her dad waiting for him to wake up. Every beat, every pulse gets slower and slower.

Eleanor: Dad? Please say something to me...

Her father still doesn't speak. The monitor machine keeps beeping, but eventually it went to a flatline. Eleanor is stricken by the sound as she didn't fully understand it.

Eleanor: Dad?... Dad?!...

She notices that his hand has lost grip of hers. Eleanor is feeling scared, and she starts tearing up again.

Eleanor: Dad?!!

No one speaks. The flatline on the machine continues. Eleanor feels heavy, time slows down. A few nurses are rushing in to help her dad. More medical staff come through with defibrillators. Her dad is surrounded by lots of staff trying to aid him. Shortly after, Kim and Cyndy return. They immediately knew something is wrong. Kim is in shock as she begins to hold her daughter back. Cyndy is screaming in silence, rushing outside the room hollering for more help. Eleanor is crying hard as she's trying to break free from her mother's arms. Everyone is trying hard to save Jonas, but all anyone can hear is still a flatline. He's gone... Kim begins crying as she holds Eleanor close. After countless tries with no luck, the nurses start unplugging the machines. All the staff clears out of the room to give them some time alone. Cyndy eyes are heavy with tears. She didn't want to believe it, no one could believe it. Kim then lets go of Eleanor so she could go see her dad. She's tightening up with her emotions and she couldn't breathe. As she walks up to him she hugs his lifeless body. His touch brought out more tears from her eyes, and she could breathe again in lament. Eleanor couldn't let go. How could she? The ache she feels inside, feeling alone for their last goodbye. But even in her time of loss, her mother is still by her side.

A couple weeks have passed, after Jonas had passed away. The angels have cried from the sky, the playgrounds are empty of all the children, the waters are streaming down from higher rivers, and the brown leaves are falling thousands from the branches. Close friends and family are all paying their respects. Everyone is dressed in suits and ties and black dresses. Flowers cut and placed aside. Jonas is buried at Alchemilla Cemetery next to his mother's grave. On his tombstone it said "Jonas Rivers born Sep. 26, 1963 died Oct. 22, 1998." Isaac's grave lies next to his along with the other ten children that were missing back from 1980. Eleanor is standing with her mother feeling weightless, numb, and sore. Apart of him in her is torn, but he's free. They're all free. She then walks up to one of the children's tombstones and places a flower on their grave. With the extra flowers they had all of them do the same after her. First Kim, second Cyndy, then Iris and her son, and Walter was last. All of the kids were given a flower to restore their innocence to create warmth and beauty for their lost souls. The living ones stand bruised but not broken with the currency of grace for the dead in the ground. They can see the colors of goodness past the scars on their skin. All of them stay for a while feeling the air through the trees from the water that the animals drink. Breathing out as the mountainside breathes them in. The year is a promise they hold as a memento mori, and a broken design they did not plan themselves.

...: After that day... For the first time, in a long time, the grey clouds have cleared from the sky letting the sun shine over Aqua Heights... The steam is finally gone... Maybe the incident from the water plant many years ago was a myth... or maybe it wasn't... Maybe it was just coincidence... But everything changed after those missing children were found... Eleanor knew where they were because of Isaac... For a long time they were all lying at the bottom of that lake in plastic bags... It's still hard to digest... I guess it always was for Isaac too... I can't imagine... My dear friend, Jonas. I remember him like yesterday... When I first walked into that bar and saw him, I was in need of a friend. I could tell he did too... I still wish things turned out differently for him... I wish he was still here... But I guess there are some things that come at a heavy price... But if they're worth it, then that cost won't matter... Death is inevitable for all of us. We'll never know when it'll come to visit us... It can be unfair sometimes, but it's always easier to accept it for ourselves than the ones we love... So hopefully, maybe we'll all see each other again in the end... Until then, I'll carry on... Although the streams are still quiet, the town is not. People are no longer anointed by fear. Their children can feel safe again. In this darkness, the light has been found... And so this is why I wrote this story, in Jonas's honor... There are still times of silence, still times of grief soaring the edifice of our lives, but happiness we can still find. With patience, home is amounted... We may or may not see what lies in our futures. But today we have today...

JONAS'S FILE:

Age: 35

Weight: 197lbs

Height: 72.0"

Hair Color: Dark Brown

ELEANOR'S FILE:

Age: 13

Weight: 93lbs

Height: 62.0"

Hair Color: Dark Brown

KIM'S FILE:

Age: 33

Weight: 120lbs

Height: 69.0"

Hair Color: Brown

CYNDY'S FILE:

Age: 35

Weight: 130lbs

Height: 69.0"

Hair Color: Dark Blonde

ZACH'S FILE:

Age: 30

Weight: 190lbs

Height: 71.0"

Hair Color: Light Brown

ISAAC'S FILE:

Age: ???

Weight: ???

Height: ???

Hair Color: ???

WALTER'S FILE:

Age: 66

Weight: 230lbs

Height: 71.0"

Hair Color: White and Grey

IRIS'S FILE:

Age: 28

Weight: 105lbs

Height: 68.0"

Hair Color: Black

Made in the USA
Columbia, SC
06 February 2022